A Name Stolen

Also by Scott E Adams

The Tales of Blowville

The Hollow Tree
The Cellar Below
The Long Return

The Charlie Randall Chronicles

A Name Stolen

A Name Stolen

The Charlie Randall Chronicles

Volume 1

Scott E Adams

Published by:
Scott Adams

ISBN 979-8-9939849-5-7

This book is dedicated to my grandson Charlie.

Table of Contents

Table of Contents (continued)

Foreword

From 1869 until the turn of the twentieth century, Potter County, Pennsylvania lived under prohibition. By law, no alcohol was to be sold, served, or manufactured within its borders. For the first two decades, the rule held with little disturbance. The county was rural, sparsely populated, and slow-moving. Men worked hard, went home early, and drank what little they could find without much fuss. There were no great scandals, no legendary shootouts, no stories that traveled far beyond the ridges.

That quiet ended in the 1890s.

The hemlock timber boom transformed the southern half of the county almost overnight. Logging companies moved in. Rail spurs were laid. Bark yards and mills rose along creeks and hollows. Hundreds of woodsmen followed the work, spending their weeks felling trees in remote camps scattered across the hills.

Cash, however, did not follow as easily.

In the forested regions of nineteenth-century, where men in lumber camps toiled to harvest the trees, many companies paid their workers not in cash, but in company scrip; a substitute for legal tender issued by the employer itself. This scrip could be exchanged only at company-owned stores, where prices were set by the same men who issued the pay.

In theory, scrip was a convenience. In practice, it shaped daily life. It bound workers to their employers, limited choice, and quietly controlled the flow of money through isolated communities. Scrip passed from hand to hand like real currency, used to settle debts, purchase supplies, and increasingly, to gamble. Its value was trusted not because it was legal, but because it was necessary.

When the weekend came, woodsmen left the camps and headed into town with scrip in their pockets and a strong desire to drink.

To meet that demand, a loose and largely unspoken network of clandestine saloons emerged across the county. Because alcohol was illegal, these operations had to remain hidden. Some concealed themselves behind legitimate businesses, restaurants, barbershops, general stores, or boarding houses, with a curtain, cellar door, or back room separating lawful commerce from unlawful indulgence. Others were little more than rough sheds erected for the sole purpose of serving whiskey out of sight of the road.

These places came to be known as pig's ears.

Pig's ears were not merely places to drink. They became the beating heart of weekend life. Gambling followed naturally, fueled by company scrip that moved across card tables as freely as coins ever had. Fighting followed too. And often, women whose livelihoods existed in the same shadows as the liquor. Money moved quickly through these rooms. So did rumors. And where law receded, power quietly filled the gap.

The towns named in this book, Galeton, Austin, Costello, Blowville, and others like them, were real places. They existed under real laws and faced real pressures brought on by rapid industrial growth, transient labor, and the strain of enforcing prohibition in a county built on isolation and hard work. Pig's ears, by name or by function, were part of that landscape, and their patrons were not always easy neighbors.

The story that follows, however, is a work of fiction.

While it draws from historical conditions, geography, and social realities of Potter County in the late nineteenth century, the characters, events, and specific circumstances portrayed here are imagined. Any resemblance to actual persons, living or deceased, is purely coincidental and unintended. This narrative is not meant to accuse, expose, or reconstruct any real individual or family history, but rather to explore the human consequences of secrecy, ambition, and survival in a place where the law and the land did not always agree.

This is a story about names, and what can be done with them.

About the things men bury and the ways they resurface. About how quiet valleys remember more than they ever say.

Welcome to the county as it stood when the trees were falling, the whiskey was hidden, the scrip passed from hand to hand, and the truth rarely stayed where it was put.

Prologue

November 12, 1898 - Blowville

The house felt wrong without Terrence Fee in it.

Not empty. Not abandoned. Just wrong. As though the walls had learned the sound of his footsteps, the rhythm of his muttering, the strange hours he kept as his mind wandered further from the world most people lived in. Without him, the silence pressed in heavy, like snow packed tight against a closed door.

Sarah Ebenspecker stood at the front window, cleaning the glass for no reason at all. Fee had never cared for tidiness. That had been one of the few steady things about him, even as his mind fractured in those last months. Sometimes he talked to shadows in the corners. Sometimes he forgot whole days. Sometimes he stood at this very window and stared at the ridge behind the house, as if something waited there for him, something only he could see.

Now he was dead, and the house still carried the weight of him, but not the warmth.

She lowered the rag and looked out over Blowville.

The town lay quiet beneath the early winter sky, cabins hunched close to Bailey Run, bark sheds dark and shuttered for the season. The pig's ears were the only places alive at this hour. At the nearer one, lantern light spilled around the door of a back room where illegal whiskey flowed into chipped mugs. Men drifted in and out, boots thick with mud, collars turned high against the wind.

Fee's house sat above it all, perched just high enough to watch the valley without ever being part of it. He had liked that. He liked knowing who came and went while remaining unseen himself.

His brother, Edwin Fee, would take the place eventually, once he finished his affairs in Harrisburg. That might be months yet. Winter roads north were slow. Until he arrived, Sarah stayed on out of respect and necessity, tending the house as she always had. Alone now, in rooms too full of memory.

She crossed the parlor. The space felt stripped, but not by death. Fee had lived simply. A worn chair by the fire. A deck of cards that never stayed in one place. A ledger he had forgotten he kept. As his mind weakened, she had managed the house without ever trying to erase the man who lived in it.

Now she gathered only what belonged to her.

Her trunk sat open on the bed in the small room she had used while working for Fee. She knelt beside it and lifted the folded scrap of ledger paper from where it rested on her shawl. The name pulled at her eye the way a nail draws a magnet.

CHARLES RANDALL — PAID IN FULL

Crane had given her the page two months earlier. She could still see him standing in the doorway well past midnight, hat in his hands, his face drawn tight in a way she had rarely seen.

"You got a place to keep something safe?" he had asked.

"Safe from who?" she had answered.

"Anyone," he said. "Everyone. I am not sure what is coming."

When he handed her the folded scrap, his fingers had trembled. Crane did not tremble. His fear usually curled inward, where no one could reach it. She had unfolded the page, taken in the ink, the neat columns, the name she did not recognize.

"What is this?" she had asked.

"Something that will matter when I am gone," Crane said. "Something Barclay will want. Something Fee might have understood once. I cannot carry it anymore."

"Why me?"

"Because you do not lie to yourself," he said. "And because you know this valley keeps its books in ink and blood both."

She had not liked the way he said it. She liked it even less now.

Fee died three weeks later.

They found the front door to the Fee Brothers mill house standing open. No sign of forced entry. No clear struggle at first. Only a lantern burned low in the hall and mud where no mud should have been, smeared along the stairs, across the walls, even the ceiling.

The cellar door hung open. And below, in the hollow beneath the floorboards, something had dug upward.

They found Terrence Fee in his study, slumped into the corner. His shirt was soaked through. A pistol lay in his hand, unfired.

Crane disappeared soon after. No explanation. No body. No word. His absence settled over Blowville like a fog that refused to lift.

Now Sarah sat with the ledger page in her hands, feeling the edges soften from being held too many times.

Paid in full.

Paid for what.

Paid by whom.

The name Charles Randall meant nothing to her. But Crane had believed the scrap mattered enough to risk leaving it with her. And the valley did not write down a stranger's name without reason.

She crossed to the loose board in the corner of the room. Her fingers found the edge and pried it up. The space beneath held only what she trusted: a cloth bundle containing her father's coroner note, a brooch that had belonged to her mother, and the list of names she had gathered in the years since George Ebenspecker died on the banks of a mountain stream with too many answers that did not fit the truth.

She slid the torn ledger page in among them.

She pressed the board back into place and stood.

From the kitchen came the faint click of a log catching in the stove. The house shifted, settling into its new silence. Sarah walked to the door and looked down toward the pig's ear, its lantern glow blurred now by falling snow.

When the roads thawed, she would begin searching again. Galeton. Austin. Costello. Wherever the name Randall led her. Wherever Crane's fear had pointed.

Someone had killed her father. Someone had broken Crane. And Charles Randall was tangled in it all.

When she found the truth, winter or summer, man or ghost, someone would answer for it.

She closed the door against the cold.

Beneath the thin floorboard in the small back room, the ledger scrap rested in the dark, where silence kept its accounts longer than most men dared.

Part 1

Galeton

1

Into Galeton

September 27, 1898 - Galeton

By the time Charlie Randall saw the smoke from Galeton's mills, the dust on his coat had settled deep into the seams and the last of his money sat folded flat inside his left boot.

He walked the road with an easy, steady pace, hat pulled low against the early autumn sun. The sky was a hard blue, the sort that made the hills appear closer than they truly were. Hemlocks leaned in on either side of the road, their dark trunks smelling of resin and old rain. Ahead, beyond the bend, came the sound of a working town. Wagon wheels groaning under weight. Hammer striking iron. Voices rising and falling in patterns shaped by labor rather than conversation.

Charlie took it in the way he took in a table. First the lay of the boards. Then the hands that would sit around it.

Company town, he thought. Lumber mills. Bark yards. Tight belts drawn around every man who lived here. Wages paid in paper instead of coin. Trouble whispered in back rooms where lantern light burned low and people pretended they were not breaking county law.

He did not mind places like that. They had rules, even when they pretended not to. He made an honest living where he could. He kept his face quiet, his hands clean, and he moved on when a town began asking the wrong kind of questions.

The road curved and Galeton opened beneath him. First the pond, flat and dark, its surface filmed with sawdust that dulled the light.

Then the long gray mill buildings, windows thrown open to haze and heat. Beyond them, houses and boarding shacks pressed close together along rutted streets. Smoke hung low, cut through by thin streams of steam from the mill stacks.

Charlie slowed at the edge of town. Watched. Measured.

A group of workers stood outside the company office, their postures stiff and guarded. Charlie drifted a little off the road and stopped beneath the shade of a young maple, where he could listen without appearing to do so.

"Short again," one of the men said.

"Promised Friday," another answered.

"You tell that to my wife," a third added, his voice flat with a kind of practiced restraint.

Footsteps sounded on the boardwalk. A deputy stepped out from the office doorway, his badge catching the sunlight.

"Easy now," the deputy called. "You boys want to keep your positions, you would do best to mind yourselves."

"We want what is owed," one of the workers said.

"You got what is owed," the deputy replied. "Any short notes get corrected on the next cycle. You know that."

"That is what they said last month."

The deputy let his hand rest at his side. Not on the gun. Just close enough to remind them it was there.

"You talk like that in front of the wrong folks," he said, "and the next cycle might skip you altogether."

The words settled in the air. Not fear, exactly. More the tired understanding of men who knew how narrow their choices were. One by one, they drifted back toward the mills, shoulders slumped, conversation finished.

The deputy scanned the street. His gaze landed on Charlie beneath the maple.

Charlie met it and gave a small nod. The sort that said he was no trouble unless someone insisted otherwise. The deputy studied him a moment longer, then turned away.

Charlie stepped off the verge and into Galeton.

He passed the company store first. Its windows displayed shirts, boots, sugar, coffee, and every other necessity a family might need, provided they were willing to buy it at prices written small and careful in chalk. Behind the counter, a clerk with a pencil tucked behind his ear tallied each sale in a ledger, never looking up as customers came and went.

Ink before mercy, Charlie thought.

Farther down the street, the smell shifted. Less mill smoke. More tobacco from pipes clenched in calloused hands. Behind one shuttered doorway he caught the thin twang of a fiddle, quick and uncertain, as though it might be silenced at any moment. A small cluster of men passed him, speaking low about a place they meant to visit after dark. A place without a sign. A place where a man had to know someone before the door would open.

That, Charlie thought, was the first honest hint of work Galeton had offered.

He moved on at an unhurried pace, noting corners and cut paths. Shadows deep enough to hide a man. Alleys that served one purpose by day and another entirely by night.

What he needed first was a room.

He found it at Barrow's Dry Goods. The painted sign above the door had faded to near nothing, but the smaller letters beneath still read: Rooms above.

He stepped inside. A bell chimed overhead.

Shelves stood neat with canned goods, folded shirts, bolts of calico. The air smelled of dust and starch. Behind the counter stood Widow Barrow, sleeves rolled, her eyes sharp enough to weigh a man before he spoke.

"You are not from the shifts," she said.

"No, ma'am."

"You in town for work or wandering."

“Neither, if I can help it,” Charlie said. “I just need a room and a quiet place to sit before I move on.”

Her gaze tightened, only slightly. “Cards.”

“Yes, ma’am.”

“Quiet cards.”

“That is the only kind I play.”

She studied him another moment, then nodded toward the back of the shop. “Stairs are behind the curtain. Third door on the right. You pay three nights in advance.”

“That is fair.”

“Two dollars and fifty.”

He placed the coins on the counter. She swept them into a tin without counting.

“Do not bring noise up those stairs,” she said.

“I am quiet by trade.”

“We will see.”

Upstairs, the room was small but clean. A narrow bed. A washstand. A chair set beside a window that looked down onto the street. Charlie sat and let his weight settle, watching the rhythm of Galeton move below him.

Men finished their shifts and spilled into the road in loose lines and clusters. None of them crossed openly toward drink or cards. Still, Charlie noticed how several glanced toward the west end of town before peeling away. Alone. Never in a group. Never with haste. Only with purpose.

He followed their path with his eyes.

Beside Barrow’s store, and the narrow building next to it, lay an alley nearly swallowed by shadow. Men slipped into it one at a time. They did not come out again, at least not by that route.

He knew the signs.

A quiet room. A door without a window. A place where someone took a little on the side if you whispered the right word.

Night settled in. Lanterns lit the road in small pools of yellow. The mill whistle blew, sharp and final. The street thinned, leaving only men with their collars turned up and their intentions kept close.

Charlie slipped his deck into his coat, checked the weight of the money in his boot, and went downstairs.

Widow Barrow did not look up as he passed the counter.

He stepped into the street with the ease of a man who had arrived in towns like this before. He let the evening close around him, moving slowly, avoiding attention, until he reached the far end of the block.

He turned down a narrow cut between two sheds, circled back, and approached the rear of Barrow's store where the alley opened into a dark pocket of space. A plain door waited there. No sign. No music. Only the faint glow of lamplight at the cracks and the low murmur of men trying not to be heard.

Charlie paused and listened.

Cards. He could always tell.

He reached for the handle, then let his hand fall. Long enough to remember that he could walk away. He had done it before. Plenty of towns never learned his name, and never would.

But he was tired. He needed work. And the valley did not often offer clean invitations.

He raised his hand and knocked.

2

The Widow's Back Room

September 27 (night), 1898 - Galeton

The knock had barely faded when a voice came through the door.

"You lost, friend?"

Charlie kept his tone mild. "Looking for a chair and a quiet game."

A pause followed. He heard a breath drawn in close, cloth shifting against wood. Then the latch clicked. The door opened just wide enough for one man to stand in the gap.

The fellow was lean and wiry, his beard gray with stubble, his eyes flattened by years of seeing too much and caring less. He looked Charlie over from hat to boots, then lingered on Charlie's hands as if weighing what they might do.

"You know where you are," the man said.

"I have an idea," Charlie replied.

"Say you are here to buy stew."

Charlie did not blink. "I am here to buy stew."

That earned the faintest twitch of a smile.

"All right then," the man said. "Keep your voice down. Keep your temper lower."

He stepped back and pulled the door open.

The Widow's back room opened like the lower half of a split crate.

Lantern light washed the space in slow yellow swells, leaving the corners half drowned in shadow. Smoke sagged low against the ceiling. Along the left wall stood a narrow plank bar where half a dozen men leaned with mugs in hand.

Their clothes told the story before their faces did. Woodsmen with sleeves rolled high, still carrying the smell of sap and sweat. Two tannery men in dark coats stained past saving. A pair of mill hands with sawdust clinging to their collars. A store clerk trying hard to look as though he belonged among them. All pretending they were not breaking county law as they tipped back mugs filled with illegal whiskey.

The scent struck Charlie first. Rotgut sharp enough to sting the nose. Grain spirit cut with molasses. Something harsher beneath it all. Whatever it was, it kept the men warm and quiet.

A few glanced up at Charlie, eyes narrowing long enough to judge whether he might bring trouble with him. Then they turned back to their drinks, shoulders drawn close, heads bent for private talk.

The gambling table sat deeper in the room. A long board balanced on sawhorses, surrounded by chairs that had long ago lost any claim to comfort. Four men were already seated. Another stood nearby, leaning against the wall with his arms crossed. At the far end, the doorman took his place behind a small counter where a few bottles stood beside a heavy lockbox.

Pinned to the wall behind him were several sheets of paper. Ledger scraps, torn from a larger book. The edges were curled, the ink faded from too many hands brushing past.

Charlie let his eyes touch them for no more than a half heartbeat before turning back to the table.

The doorman nodded toward an empty chair.

"Buy in is one dollar to sit," he said. "Money goes to the house. The rest is yours if you can walk out with it."

Charlie set a dollar on the counter. The doorman swept it away and gave a single nod.

"You play now," he said. Then louder, for the benefit of the men at the bar, "Table is clean."

It was not clean. No pig's ear ever was. But the words served their purpose.

Charlie took the seat with his back to the side wall. From there he could see the table and most of the bar without turning his head. A cluster of woodsmen drank from shared mugs, their voices low, eyes lifting whenever the door creaked or a bootstep passed outside.

The men at the table paid them little mind. Regulars, by the look of them. Here as much for the cards as for the whiskey.

Across from Charlie, the clerk with the neat collar cut a glance toward the bar. "Busy for a Monday," he muttered.

"That spill up at the north mill has folks rattled," the logger beside him said. "Men drink more when they are rattled."

"Men drink more when they are breathing," the doorman said.

Charlie picked up his first hand. Nothing to speak of. He folded without comment. The table barely noticed.

But he did.

The logger's hands were thick and square, scarred from years of work. The nervous man beside him breathed through his mouth, staring too long at each card as it came down. The quiet fellow with the fine shirt beneath his work coat played only when the pot had grown heavy enough to be worth the risk.

Behind them, the bar filled further. More woodsmen arrived, shoulders stooped from the day. A railway man slipped in through the alley door, took a fast swallow, and left again without lingering. Two younger bark peelers whispered with their heads nearly touching, casting glances toward the table as though they were unsure whether to approach it or keep their distance.

The room carried a charge that only illegal places held. Whiskey softened voices but sharpened instincts. Beneath every swallow lingered the thought of a deputy's knock.

Charlie knew rooms like this. Improvised, hidden, but governed by rules no one spoke aloud.

The next hand came. Charlie stayed in, lost small, and kept his posture easy.

A woodsman at the bar glanced toward the table and muttered, "That the new one."

"Looks like it," his companion said. "Plays too calm."

"Calm gets you killed quicker than whiskey," the first man replied before draining his mug.

The doorman shot them a look. They fell silent.

After a few rounds, the room shifted. Not louder. Just tighter. Whiskey worked through blood and bone. Cards worked at nerves already worn thin. The doorman moved steadily through his bottle, pouring short cups for men who bought favor as quietly as they bought drink.

The logger leaned toward Charlie after folding a hand. "You play like a man with nothing to lose."

Charlie kept his eyes on the table. "I play what is in front of me."

"That so," the logger said. "We had another man in here talked like that once. Did not go well for him."

"Reuben," the nervous man hissed. "Leave it alone."

"I am only talking," Reuben said. "Place like this, talking is cheap."

The clerk tapped his stack of scrip. "Not always."

Charlie let it pass. He had learned long ago when a room wanted a man to rise and when it wanted him to stay low among the whispers.

A hand later, the table shifted again. Charlie won a modest pot. The logger studied him openly now. The clerk measured him with care. Even the drinkers at the bar fell quiet long enough to look his way.

People drank here. People gambled here. But more than that, they watched. A pig's ear never stopped watching.

Charlie lifted his next hand and let the tension settle around him like smoke caught beneath lantern glass.

There was something else in the room. Something that moved between the ledger scraps on the wall and the future-dated scrip stacked at the clerk's elbow. He could feel it working, quiet and patient.

He did not yet know what the connection was.

But he knew this much.

The Widow's back room was not only a place to drink what the law forbade.

It was a place where someone kept score.

And someone was waiting to see how Charlie Randall fit into the count.

3

A Tense Table

September 27 (late night), 1898 - Galeton

The deeper the night sank, the tighter the room drew around the table. Lantern light settled low and thick, turning every face partly into shadow. Smoke crawled toward the cracks in the boards overhead, where faint sounds from the store above seeped through. Outside, the street had gone quiet, broken only by the occasional boots passing on packed dirt.

Inside the Widow's back room, tension no longer simmered. It steeped.

Charlie sat with his back to the wall, fingers resting lightly on the cards before him, breathing slow and even. The rhythm of betting had changed. Small talk faded away. Wins and losses no longer felt incidental. They felt personal.

It began with Reuben Clancy.

Charlie had not known the man's name until someone muttered it under his breath, but it fit the shape of him. Broad shoulders. A jaw like a millstone. Hands that looked as though they had been carved from bark. A logger, and one accustomed to being deferred to.

Clancy had played tight at first. Careful. Watching Charlie more than the cards. Then he lost a little too much. Then he began pressing, trying to claw it back in ways that made the table uneasy.

"You sure that is how you meant to bet it," Clancy said, nudging two folded pieces of scrip forward with his thumb. "Seems light for a man holding anything worth looking at."

His voice was calm, but there was an edge beneath it. One that suggested the hand mattered less than the challenge.

Charlie kept his eyes on the cards. "I play what I have."

"You play like you know too much," Clancy said.

"Or not enough," Charlie replied.

A few men shifted in their chairs. Not loud. Not dramatic. Enough to mark the moment. A logger pushed toward a line in a room where pride had nowhere safe to go.

The clerk with the neat stacks of scrip began tapping his finger faster than before. The nervous man across from him had stopped blinking altogether.

The doorman drifted closer to the table, pretending to straighten mugs at the counter.

The enforcer pushed off the wall and stood a little straighter.

Clancy drew in a breath through his nose, slow and deliberate, then let it out through his teeth. "Go on then," he said. "Show me."

Charlie lifted the corners of his cards just enough to look. Three jacks. Two nines. A full house. Strong, but not unbeatable. He did not reveal it.

His eyes stayed on Clancy. "You first."

The logger shoved his bet in deeper. Too deep for the hand he held. The desperation was in the weight of the move, not in his face.

Charlie matched it without hesitation and laid his cards on the table.

For a moment Clancy only stared. Not shocked. More stunned that someone had stepped cleanly through a bluff he believed was hidden.

He turned his cards over.

A pair of tens.

A low murmur passed around the room before anyone could stop it.

Clancy shoved his chair back hard enough to jostle a lantern. "You should not have called me on that."

“You gave me reason to,” Charlie said.

Clancy rose halfway from his seat, palms pressed flat against the table. The enforcer took a single step forward, slow and unmistakable, placing himself at Clancy’s side.

The doorman leaned in. “Sit down, Reuben.”

Clancy did not look away from Charlie. His jaw tightened. His neck flushed red. Then the stillness of the room reached him. The danger was too close, too plain.

He eased back into his chair. The motion carried no ease with it.

The enforcer remained where he was, arms crossed once more.

Charlie gathered the pot and stacked it with quiet care. Every movement measured. Nothing showy. Nothing that could be mistaken for triumph.

He had played enough rooms to know when winning itself became a risk.

A few hands passed before Charlie noticed a different strain settling in. Not on the table, but behind it.

The clerk leaned toward the nervous man and whispered, “We do not mention the last gambler who asked too much.”

The nervous man flinched. “Shut your mouth.”

“I am just saying,” the clerk replied. “There are questions better left alone.”

Charlie studied his cards, but his hearing sharpened.

Last gambler. Asked too much.

He drew a slow breath. He had heard whispers like that before. Not here. Elsewhere. Towns where men vanished into trees, into debts, or into the wrong side of a cellar door.

Across the table, Clancy rubbed the back of his neck. “Nobody needs to talk about that.”

The doorman’s voice cut in sharp. “Play.”

Cards were dealt again. Charlie forced his attention back to the game.

This hand told him the table had shifted once more. No longer toward violence, but toward caution. Men watched him more closely now. Watched one another. Watched the door.

Watched the ledger scraps pinned behind the counter, their edges curled from handling.

The scribbled numbers. The names. The careful columns that did not belong in a room like this.

The clerk had stopped tapping. His eyes were fixed on Charlie.

"You win quiet," he said. "But you win a little too clean."

Charlie lifted a brow. "You prefer I win messy?"

The clerk did not smile. "Men who read a table that well tend to read other things too."

"I read what is in front of me," Charlie said.

"Do you," the clerk asked, "or do you read behind it."

The doorman shot him a warning look. The clerk fell silent.

Play continued, but the game had thinned to gestures. Bets slid forward without comment. Every movement cautious. Even the lantern hiss sounded louder than it had before.

Charlie played three more hands. He lost two on purpose. Let the room cool around him again like banked coals.

Then the doorman spoke. "Night has run long enough. House is closing."

It was early. Every man at the table knew it.

But the rule was just as clear. When a pig's ear doused a fire, it meant someone did not like how bright it had begun to burn.

Chairs scraped. Coins clinked. Men rose.

Charlie pocketed his modest winnings without haste, making each motion look ordinary.

Clancy watched him go.

The clerk watched him go.

The enforcer watched him most of all.

At the door, the doorman caught Charlie's sleeve just long enough to speak through touch alone. "Leave quiet," he murmured. "And do not turn down the alley. Someone might think you are looking for answers."

Charlie nodded once and stepped into the cooler night air.

The door closed behind him with a soft, final click.

Charlie walked into the dark street as the town settled toward sleep. His thoughts did not settle with it.

One phrase kept circling his mind, tight and sharp.

The last gambler who asked too much.

He did not yet know whose name it belonged to.

But he had the sense that, before long, someone would try to make sure Charlie Randall learned the cost of asking.

4

A Week in Galeton

September 28, 1898 - Galeton

Charlie woke the next morning to the steady hum of the mill and the faint smell of starch rising from Widow Barrow's shop below. Sunlight pushed through the narrow window of his room, catching dust motes that drifted in the beams like slow-falling ash.

He sat on the edge of the bed for a moment, listening to wagons creak past in the street. The Widow's back room had given him a seat at the table, but it would not teach him the town. A gambler learned a place by walking it, not by hiding inside a single room.

He stepped out onto Main Street with his hat pulled low against the glare.

Galeton looked different in daylight. Less secretive, but no less burdened. Men queued outside the company office, waiting their turn to argue short wages. A woman hurried past with her shawl drawn tight, eyes fixed ahead. A barking dog chased two children across the yard behind a boarding house until a voice called them back.

Charlie passed through it all without drawing notice.

He followed Pine Creek north, where the water murmured dark and cold beneath a plank bridge. A few woodsmen smoked along the bank, passing a tin cup between them. They watched him with neither welcome nor suspicion, only the guarded indifference of men accustomed to strangers moving through the valley.

"Morning," Charlie said.

The tallest of them nodded once. "You the card man from the widow's place."

Charlie paused. "Word travels quick."

The man shrugged. "Not much else does."

They let the silence sit a moment. Then Charlie moved on.

He spent the day learning how Galeton breathed. How the mill whistle cut the hours clean. How men shifted at the sound of it. How the deputy lingered near the company store longer than honest business required, hands loose, eyes always moving.

As evening settled in, Charlie slipped into a narrow lane behind the blacksmith's shop where a rough table rested on two barrels. Three loggers stood there, passing a bottle wrapped in paper.

One of them eyed him. "Looking to buy a swallow."

Charlie shook his head. "Just passing."

"Suit yourself," the man said, lifting the bottle. "Town goes dry by law, but we keep a little wet for ourselves."

Charlie kept walking, noting which doors stayed slightly ajar, which windows were masked with blankets to hide lantern glow, which sheds drew men one at a time after dark.

A pig's ear was not the only place to drink in a dry county. That was part of what made valleys like this uneasy. Too many shadows. Too many men who claimed them.

By the third evening, Charlie had a lay of the land.

He knew the cleanest path from the Widow's store to the riverbank without crossing the deputy's usual patrol. He knew which alleys offered cover and which were watched. He knew the mill foreman kept an arrangement in a butcher's cellar on the south side of town. He knew the men who drank hardest at night arrived for their shifts an hour early, hoping to sweat their secrets out before daylight.

He knew enough to move without drawing eyes.

On the fourth night, he returned to the Widow's back room but did not take a chair at the table. He stood back and watched. Watched

Reuben Clancy's temper simmer beneath his heavy breathing. Watched the clerk slip a piece of scrip aside when he thought no one noticed. Watched the doorman handle the bottle with care, pouring for some men and turning others away without explanation.

A man at the bar wore a tannery apron and shook slightly as he drank, eyes fixed on his mug as though waiting for courage to settle in.

The doorman caught Charlie's gaze. "Quiet night," he said.

Charlie nodded. "Seems that way."

"Might stay so if folks mind their business."

"Do I look like a man looking for trouble?"

"Not yet."

Charlie left before midnight, stepping into cool air thick with fog rising off the run. Lanterns glowed behind curtained windows. A woman's voice carried through the dusk as she scolded a child. The valley felt close around him, listening.

On the fifth morning, Charlie paid for another day. Widow Barrow counted the coins one by one, her eyes never leaving him.

"You planning on settling," she asked.

"No, ma'am. Just staying until I earn enough to move quiet."

"You cause any ruckus in my rooms."

"I aim to stay a ghost."

She snorted softly. "Ghosts do not rent rooms for long."

Charlie allowed himself a small smile.

By the sixth night, Charlie noticed something else. The ledger scraps pinned behind the counter were never moved. No new names appeared. No marks were erased. Yet the doorman checked them often, running his thumb slowly down the ink as though testing memory against what had been written.

Charlie drank a single cup of the illegal whiskey that night. It burned like pine resin cut with vinegar, but it warmed him enough to dull the fog-bound chill that crept in from the river.

He asked about the ledger scraps the same way he asked about everything. Offhand. As if it barely mattered.

The man behind the bar paused mid-wipe. He did not answer right away. He set the rag down, wiped his hands on his apron, and kept his eyes on the wood.

"Ledgers," he said at last. "That is not the kind of thing you ask about in town."

"Why not," Charlie said.

The man's mouth twitched, not quite a smile. "Because men do not get fired for asking questions like that."

He picked up the rag again and walked to the far end of the bar.

"They just stop showing up."

* * *

On the seventh morning, before the mills fully woke, Charlie came down the narrow stairs and found Widow Barrow sweeping her porch.

She looked up. "Your three nights are done."

"I was hoping to stay another week."

"Five dollars."

Charlie blinked. "Five."

"You want cheaper, you can sleep in the hay under the rail spur. Rats charge more than I do."

He reached into his boot, withdrew folded bills, and placed them in her hand.

She nodded once. "Room stays yours. Keep quiet, keep clear of the deputy, and do not ask questions meant for other men."

"I make a habit of that."

"I hope so. Town has a memory."

She stepped aside to let him pass.

Charlie climbed the stairs again, her words settling with weight. Galeton did have a memory. The men at the back room table had made that plain. Someone before him had asked too much. Someone before him had walked these streets and ended up on the wrong side of the ledger.

He set his hat on the washstand, sat on the bed, and rubbed the bridge of his nose.

He had planned to stay three days, not seven. Planned to play cards, not listen for danger in every alley. But the valley had drawn him in, step by step, card by card. Now he felt something shifting around him. Quiet. Certain.

He had paid for another week.

And he would need every day of it to understand why Galeton was watching him so closely.

5

The Big Win

October 4 (evening), 1898 - Galeton

By the time the mills blew for the late shift's end, Charlie knew the night would run hard.

The air carried the weight of it. Clouds pressed low against the ridge, holding the day's heat in the valley. Pine Creek moved dark and slow. Men coming off the line walked with their shoulders set tight, the posture of short pay and promises made for the next cycle instead of tonight.

Charlie watched them drift past Widow Barrow's storefront from the upstairs window. Some went straight home. Some paused to speak in low, angry voices. A few peeled away without comment and slipped toward the alley at the back.

Toward the pig's ear.

He drew the curtain and stood for a moment in the dimness of his room. He checked the weight in his boot, then his pocket, where a thin stack of coins and scrip rested. Not much. Enough to buy a seat. Not enough to recover from a careless night.

Charlie picked up his deck and shuffled once, listening to the soft slap of paper against paper.

Tonight, he thought, would show him what Galeton was really holding.

He went down the narrow stairs. Widow Barrow stood behind the counter, counting change. She did not look at him, but her words found him all the same.

"Back rooms stay quiet," she said.

"That is how I like them," Charlie replied.

"You win too much in a town like this," she said, "somebody notices."

"Then I will try not to be memorable."

She gave a soft snort, as though she did not believe such a thing could be helped.

Out back, the alley smelled of damp wood and coal smoke. Lantern light traced the edges of the door. Charlie knocked twice, then once more, the pattern he had been taught.

The doorman opened the door a crack, then swung it wider. "Evening," he said. "Stew again?"

"Stew."

Inside, the back room was crowded. Lanterns burned low, but not low enough to hide the number of men packed along the plank bar. Woodsmen with wet cuffs. Tannery men with stained hands. A pair of railroad workers leaning close over a shared bottle. Mugs lifted and lowered in a steady rhythm. Laughter came in short bursts and died just as quickly.

The outlaw whiskey moved faster than the words.

The table was full. Reuben Clancy sat in his usual place, shoulders squared, jaw set. The nervous man faced him, eyes already dulled by drink. The clerk with the neat stacks of scrip had his collar open and sleeves rolled, as if he had decided to belong to the room tonight. The quiet fellow with the fine shirt beneath his work coat sat with a modest pile, alert and patient.

The enforcer leaned against the wall, arms crossed, eyes half lidded and missing nothing.

The doorman nodded toward the table. "We have a seat if you bring a stake."

Charlie stepped to the counter and counted out his buy in. The doorman slid a small stack back to him and tipped his chin toward the chair beside Clancy.

"Luck has been thin tonight," he said. "Maybe you break it. Maybe it breaks you."

A few men chuckled.

Charlie took his seat with his back to the side wall. The room's rhythm closed around him. Cards snapped. Coins clinked. The low murmur of drinkers drifted from the bar. Somewhere above, the shop bell rang faintly through the floorboards.

The first hands told him enough. Clancy had been drinking, but not enough to dull his hands. The nervous man chased losses. The clerk chose his moments carefully. The quiet fellow played little and watched much.

Charlie played tight. Lost small. Won smaller. He let them remember him as cautious, not hungry.

Whiskey loosened tongues at the bar. Talk turned from pay to grievances, from grievances to what a man might do if he were pushed far enough. The doorman poured shorter measures as the room warmed.

After an hour, the cards turned.

Charlie picked up a hand that carried weight. Queens. Nine. Seven. Five. He stayed in and drew two. The queens paired. Four of a kind. Too strong to announce. Too rare to waste.

The pot began small. The nervous man folded early, rubbing at his temple. The quiet fellow stayed in a moment longer, then bowed out with a slight shake of his head. The clerk followed, tapping his stack as if counting ahead.

Clancy pushed in a bit more than the pot asked for. Enough to say he liked his hand.

"You have been careful all week, Randall," he said. "Maybe tonight we see what you are holding."

"Maybe," Charlie said.

He called. The clerk hesitated, then matched.

The bets came around again. Coins, then scrip. The clerk's tidy pile thinned. Clancy's breathing grew heavier. Men at the bar turned to watch.

"Man might think you work off a script," Clancy said. "Lose a little. Win a little. Then come in strong when it counts."

"I do not write things down," Charlie replied. "I leave that to company men."

A murmur passed through the drinkers. The clerk's jaw tightened.

Clancy shoved in his last coin. The clerk followed with what he could. All eyes turned to Charlie.

He looked at the pot. At the men watching him. At Clancy's jaw working as though chewing on something hard.

Charlie slid his full stack forward.

The nervous man let out a short whistle. "That is a pot."

"Or trouble," the quiet fellow said.

"Show it," Clancy said.

The clerk laid his hand down first. A full house. Kings over nines. Strong enough most nights.

Clancy slapped his cards down next. A flush, neat and high.

"Beat that," he said.

Charlie placed his four queens gently between them.

The room went still.

Lantern light caught the sweat along Clancy's temple. The clerk's face went slack, then smoothed itself blank. For a moment, Charlie thought the logger might come across the table.

Then the enforcer spoke, calm and final. "Hand is played."

Clancy's fists clenched, then opened.

Charlie gathered the pot carefully. Coins first. Then scrip.

As his fingers brushed the paper, something caught his eye.

The print. Goodyear. The dates.

He turned one slip as though checking its value. PAYROLL, stamped across the top. Dated two weeks ahead.

Another piece matched it.

He did not let his face change.

"You paying in company scrip now, Reuben," someone at the bar called.

"Money is money," Clancy snapped.

"Not when it is not supposed to be here yet," the clerk muttered, too low for most to hear.

Charlie heard.

He folded the scrip into his stack, pulse tightening in his throat as his mind turned the details over. Goodyear payroll. Dated ahead. Already moving through a pig's ear before the mill men had seen a cent.

He had stepped into trouble larger than a logger's temper.

Clancy shoved his chair back. "House gets a drink on me," he said, flicking his last coin toward the bar. "I am done."

The doorman caught it and poured two short cups instead of one.

Clancy drank, then shouldered his way toward the door. He stopped beside Charlie's chair.

"You walk careful with that," he said. "Some men will not like where it came from."

"I won it fair."

"That is not the part that matters."

He left.

The room's noise returned in cautious layers. The nervous man laughed too loud and said he ought to quit while he still had boots. The clerk gathered what remained of his stake and studied Charlie with narrowed eyes.

"Luck sits strange on some men," he said.

"Cards fall how they fall."

"You notice anything particular about what you won."

"Only that I need to find someone who will take it."

"You will not have to look far."

The enforcer leaned in as if checking the house's comfort. His eyes dropped to the scrip, then lifted to Charlie.

"Keep that close," he said. "Do not wave it where certain eyes might see."

Charlie slid the Goodyear scrip into his inner pocket, feeling the stiff paper and the weight of ink that should not yet exist.

He played a few more hands, lost deliberately, and let the table cool around him. Then he stood, nodded once to the doorman, and stepped into the night.

The alley felt colder now. Fog pooled low, blurring the lights along the street.

Charlie paused, listening to the murmur from the store front, the distant grind of the mill, the soft splash of the run beyond the houses.

In his pocket, future dated scrip pressed against his chest.

Men in this valley worked a month to earn those slips of paper. Someone had found a way to move them early, to push them through back rooms before they touched a pay line.

And for reasons he did not yet understand, whoever controlled that stream did not mind Reuben Clancy holding a handful of it in a pig's ear.

Or they did not know.

Or they would know soon.

Charlie started back toward his room, keeping to shadow where he could. He had done better than planned. But the win felt less like fortune and more like a door opening onto a room he was not sure he wanted to enter.

He had come to Galeton looking for a quiet table and enough money to move on.

Instead, the valley had placed a different stake in his hand.

Ink. Dates. And a name not yet spoken, but already stirring beneath the town like something waiting to be turned over.

Charlie walked on, boots soft on packed dirt, the weight of stolen time pressed close against his heart.

6

Clancy's Rage

October 5, 1898 - Galeton

Charlie woke before sunrise, not because he meant to, but because something from the night had followed him into sleep. A memory of Clancy's face, perhaps. Or the feel of the Goodyear scrip in his pocket, stiff with danger. He lay still until the mills began to stir, then dressed and stepped out into the cool morning.

Galeton at dawn felt honest. Smoke had not yet risen. Streets lay quiet. Men had not had time to grow angry. Charlie walked with his hands in his coat, turning over the cards, the scrip, and the enforcer's warning.

By midmorning, the calm had thinned. Workers clustered outside the company office, voices sharp as saw teeth. Someone argued about short pay from the last cycle. A foreman barked back. Two men edged toward blows until the deputy stepped in, one hand resting near his belt.

Charlie kept to the margins. He had no place in any crowd.

The day wore on. He ate a small lunch from Widow Barrow's shelves, then walked the banks of Pine Creek. The valley leaned close with a waiting hush. He could not shake the sense that last night's win had brought him into view of eyes he had not yet seen.

By late afternoon the air had warmed again. Humidity gathered. Clouds thickened overhead. Charlie returned toward his room, meaning to rest before dusk.

He did not make it through the door.

A heavy footstep sounded behind him. Then another.

"You got a minute, Randall."

Charlie turned.

Reuben Clancy stood at the far end of the porch, shoulders filling the space between the posts. His shirt clung with sweat. His jaw was set hard. In his fist, crushed tight enough to crease it, was a piece of scrip.

Future dated scrip.

Charlie did not move. "Evening, Reuben."

"Do not smooth talk me," Clancy snapped. "You cheated."

"You had a good hand," Charlie said evenly. "Just not good enough."

Clancy took a step forward. The boards creaked.

"You think I am mad about losing," he said, voice low and tight. "I have lost before. Men lose. That is cards. But this." He shook the scrip once. "This is trouble."

Charlie stayed quiet.

Clancy twisted the paper in his fist. "You do not win company pay two weeks early unless you know something. Unless you are mixed in with someone."

"I know cards," Charlie said. "That is all."

"That is a lie."

Two men lingered near the road, pretending at conversation. Their eyes stayed fixed on the porch. Word of the confrontation had carried fast.

Charlie lowered his voice. "You played proud, Reuben. That is all that happened."

"Do not talk down to me."

Charlie saw the coil of temper tightening in the man's shoulders. It was never the noise that mattered. It was the quiet before it.

"I won a clean hand," Charlie said. "House saw it. You saw it."

Clancy stepped closer, close enough that Charlie caught the sour edge of whiskey on his breath. “Clean,” Clancy said, tasting the word. “A clean hand does not leave me holding this.”

He opened his fist. The scrip unfolded in the damp air.

“Where it came from is not on me,” Charlie said.

“That is exactly the point,” Clancy growled. “I did not get it from the company. And neither did you.”

Charlie felt the shift then. Clancy was not alone in his anger. Someone had spoken to him. Someone had whispered that the scrip was wrong. Someone had decided where blame should land before Charlie ever stepped onto the porch.

Clancy loomed over him. “Tell me who handed you the stack. Who told you to take my money. Who you work for.”

“Nobody.”

“That is a lie,” Clancy said, and his voice cracked. “And I am done hearing lies.”

His fist clenched again, this time empty of paper. Charlie stepped back, turning his shoulder just enough to give himself room.

Two more men had drifted closer. Whispering.

“Clancy is going to break him in half,” one said.

“This will not end quiet,” another murmured.

Charlie raised his hands slightly. Not surrender. Warning. “Think it through.”

“I have,” Clancy said.

He lunged.

Charlie slipped aside. Clancy’s fist slammed into a porch post with a dull thud. Pain flashed across the logger’s knuckles, but he swung again. Charlie ducked. The blow cut close to his ear.

A voice called from across the road. “Reuben, hold up.”

Clancy did not stop.

He grabbed Charlie's coat. Cloth twisted tight. Charlie struck Clancy's forearm, breaking the grip long enough to pivot free. They staggered apart.

"You stole from the wrong man," Clancy growled.

"I stole nothing."

Clancy charged again, full weight behind him.

Charlie moved sideways. Clancy rushed past and slammed into the railing. The wood groaned. For a moment, Charlie thought it might give way.

Clancy turned, panting, sweat streaking his brow.

"You are hiding something," he said. "That scrip is rotten, and you are standing in the middle of it."

"If it is wrong," Charlie said, "ask the man who put it in the pot."

"Do not get clever with me."

A voice cut through the heat. "That is enough."

The deputy stepped onto the porch, hand near his belt. His eyes moved between them, then settled on Clancy.

"You want to cool off in the lockup tonight," he asked.

"He cheated," Clancy said.

"No arrests over card losses," the deputy replied. "Not unless someone ends up cut."

Clancy's anger still burned, but he backed off half a step. It was not surrender. It was restraint forced by consequence.

"This is not over," he muttered.

"It is for tonight," the deputy said.

Clancy spit into the dirt and stormed off the porch, shoulders heaving as he crossed the street.

The deputy turned to Charlie. "You start that."

"Only thing I started was a win."

The deputy studied him. “Men here got short fuses. You keep winning, someone might decide they do not like how you hold your cards.”

“Then I will watch my hands.”

“I will be watching them too.”

The silence held.

Then the deputy stepped away, boots steady in the dust.

Charlie stood alone. The air had thickened again, carrying rain and the heavier scent of trouble rising through the valley.

The Goodyear scrip in his pocket felt heavier than coin.

He went inside, climbed the stairs, and shut the door.

Clancy’s rage had not come from losing a hand.

It had come from fear.

Fear of holding something he should never have touched. Fear of what it meant that Charlie had touched it too. Fear of whose name might sit behind the ink.

Charlie sat on the edge of the bed, thoughts tightening.

Someone was already watching him. Someone who knew the scrip was wrong. Someone who did not want an outsider holding pieces of a crime not yet uncovered.

He drew a slow breath.

He had come to Galeton for cards.

What he had found was a web.

And someone had already begun to pull the line he stood on.

7

The Deputy's Ultimatum

October 6 (morning), 1898 - Galeton

Rain had come in the night, tapping against the window of Charlie's rented room until the boards swelled and the smell of damp pine crept into the air. He woke early, restless, the remnants of sleep breaking apart around the memory of the porch fight. Clancy's rage had burned hot, but that was not what stayed with him. What lingered was the fear beneath it. The stiffness in the man's voice. The way his eyes had searched Charlie's face for answers he did not want to hear.

Scrip dated two weeks ahead. Men whispering. Eyes turning.

Something in Galeton had shifted its weight.

By midmorning the clouds began to lift. Charlie stepped out with his coat collar raised against the leftover drizzle. The road was soft beneath his boots, darkened by rain. Men moved about their chores with less noise than usual, glancing at him and then looking away, as though deciding whether he was worth remembering or better left alone.

He walked the length of Main Street, trying to loosen the feeling of being measured. He passed the company office, the boarding houses, the sheds stacked with bark. Eventually his feet carried him back toward the widow's store. The curtain hung still. No lookout stood near the door. But Charlie had learned enough in the past week to know that a place did not need visible eyes to watch.

He pushed through the narrow side door.

Inside, the pig's ear felt altered from two nights earlier. Smoke lay thicker, hanging low and stale. Lantern light cast a dull glow across faces that had sharpened with attention. Woodsmen lined the short counter, hands wrapped around chipped mugs, shoulders drawn in as if guarding their drink from more than the cold.

Charlie nodded to no one in particular and moved toward the table at the back.

The game ran small. A few men drifted over. Others hovered just long enough to see him, then chose different corners. Charlie caught the change immediately. Men who had spoken easily before now watched from the edges, their whispers moving across the room like loose change passed hand to hand.

"That is him," a logger muttered.

"You think he still has it," another asked.

A third voice answered low. "Future paper. Company does not like that."

Charlie kept his play tight. Conservative hands. Modest bets. He won small and lost small, letting nothing spike. His face stayed steady while the room tracked every motion. How he stacked his chips. How long his fingers rested on the cards. The quiet rhythm of his breath.

He felt it clearly now. Rumor spreading like spilled lamp oil, soaking into places it could not be gathered back up.

Someone had talked about Clancy's scrip.

Someone had talked about Charlie.

By late afternoon, Clancy still had not appeared. His empty chair carried its own weight. Men glanced at it, then back at Charlie, as if expecting trouble to choose a new shape.

Charlie cashed out after a short win and stood.

A few faces turned away too quickly. Others stared without apology. He slipped out through the back and into the cool evening air. The wind carried tannery smoke and something sharper beneath it. A warning folded into the ordinary sounds of the town.

He did not return that night.

Instead, he stayed in his room, listening to the creak of Widow Barrow's floorboards, the distant murmur of voices along the street, the soft patter of rain returning after dusk. When sleep came, it did not stay long.

* * *

Morning brought clearer skies and a sharper cold.

Charlie crossed to the small restaurant beside the mill office, where steam clouded the windows and the smell of eggs and grease drifted into the street. Inside, he ate without hurry. Men murmured over their plates. No one sat near him. The empty spaces felt deliberate.

When he finished, he stepped outside and straightened his coat.

The deputy waited across the road.

Boots set wide. Hands idle, but close enough to his belt to matter. His hat sat low, eyes shaded.

"Randall," he said.

Charlie stopped. "Deputy."

"You had yourself a busy night or two." The deputy's voice stayed even, almost courteous. "Men have been talking."

"Men always talk."

"Not like this." The deputy stepped closer. "I hear you been winning unusual paper. Company scrip that has no business moving through town yet."

Charlie let the silence stretch.

"I do not care if you win a hand," the deputy went on. "But I care when fists start flying on porches and your name comes up tied to it. Makes me look like I am not minding the fences."

"Clancy came at me."

"And I am not disputing that." The deputy nodded once. "But fights like that do not happen without reason behind them. And this one had reason written plain."

He looked Charlie over slowly.

"You want to tell me where that scrip came from."

"It came from the table," Charlie said. "Clancy put it in the pot."

The deputy held his gaze.

"You walk careful with that answer," he said. "If that paper is stolen, or forged, or meant for hands other than yours, then every man tied to it stands to lose more than a little blood."

"I won it fair."

"That is not the question." The deputy stepped close enough that Charlie caught the smell of tobacco and damp wool. "The question is why trouble followed you the moment you set foot here."

Charlie did not answer.

After a moment, the deputy straightened and adjusted his hat.

"This is how it goes," he said. "You have until sunrise tomorrow to leave Galeton. Men are on edge. The mill office is prickled up over missing accounts. And I am not spending my week breaking up fights over company paper."

The words settled heavy.

"You walk out on your own," the deputy added. "Or you stay, and I lock you up for disturbing the peace. Either way, you are gone."

He paused, then leaned in again.

"And whatever you think you are mixed in with, leave it behind. This valley has teeth when strangers start stirring the wrong pot."

He turned and walked off without waiting for a reply.

Charlie watched him go. Morning light washed over the street. Somewhere, the mills had already begun their grind.

The scrip in his pocket felt heavier than before, like a stone drawing him down.

He had known trouble before. But this was different.

Here, trouble was not reacting to him.

It was moving ahead of him.

And someone had already carried his name into places where it did not belong.

8

Forced Departure

October 6 (afternoon), 1898 - Galeton

Charlie spent the rest of the morning walking the length of Galeton, trying to settle his thoughts. The deputy's ultimatum clung to him like damp wool. Some men gave him a wide berth as he passed. Others watched openly, whispering into turned collars. The town felt wired, every exchange carrying a spark that might catch if given the chance.

By noon, he had made up his mind.

He would leave quietly, without stirring anything more than the dust his boots kicked up. Galeton had made its decision. Whether he had earned the trouble or merely stepped into it no longer mattered.

Back at Widow Barrow's place, he packed what little he owned. Shirts folded with the practiced efficiency of a man used to leaving before he was asked twice. He checked his pockets once, then again, making sure nothing was left behind that might invite questions later. The scrip stayed hidden, pressed flat and tight.

The widow lingered in the doorway, fingers worrying the hem of her apron.

"You heading out sooner than planned," she said.

"Looks that way."

She nodded, not surprised. "Clancy's still angry."

"So I hear."

Charlie closed his satchel and cinched the strap. "I will settle what I owe."

"You already paid your week," she said. "Just leave the room as you found it. And mind the road." Her eyes lifted to his, sharp and knowing. "Folks say the deputy is watching."

Charlie thanked her, shouldered his satchel, and stepped out into the afternoon.

The sky hung low, heavy with the promise of more rain. The mill whistle had sounded not long before, and workers trickled back toward their posts. Even those too busy to look his way seemed to feel the shift, the way a valley does when something unwelcome passes through it.

Charlie kept to the east road, moving with purpose but not haste. He meant to be gone before anyone decided he owed them a word.

He almost managed it.

Near the road beyond the hardware store, two men stood beside a wagon, hands busy with a harness that did not need tending. They were the same ones who had watched the porch fight days earlier. When Charlie drew close, one leaned toward the other.

"That him," he said, just loud enough. "Randall."

The other spat into the dirt. "Tell Barclay the Randall man is leaving early."

Charlie did not break stride, but his shoulders tightened.

Barclay.

The name meant nothing to him, but the way it was spoken did. Not rumor. Not idle talk. It carried the weight of someone whose notice mattered.

Charlie kept his eyes forward. The men did not follow. They did not need to. Whatever message they carried would reach its mark soon enough.

The road out of Galeton curved beside the creek, rutted and soft from wagons. As he cleared the last houses, he glanced back once. The town was already shrinking, roofs folding into one another, smoke rising thin and gray. He could feel eyes on him still, measuring the distance he put between himself and the valley.

Not all of them friendly.

He walked until the houses thinned to scattered sheds, then paused on a low rise overlooking the run. The afternoon breeze carried the sharp tang of tannins from the mills. Birds stirred in the hemlocks. Life continued without him, untroubled by his leaving.

He drew a slow breath and adjusted the satchel strap on his shoulder.

Galeton did not owe him anything. And he owed it nothing in return. But someone here, someone tied to that scrip, had taken notice. Someone had spoken his name with intent, not curiosity.

That was not trouble he could outrun forever. But distance would buy time. And time was often all a man like him had.

He turned south, toward Austin. The sky darkened as he went, hills turning blue gray as the light thinned. Behind him, the valley settled into dusk, holding the echoes of a fight he had not started and a scheme he had stepped into blind.

Charlie walked on.

Bootsteps steady. Eyes forward.

Still, the sense of being watched followed him, a shadow that did not belong to the failing light.

The widow's words returned to him, quiet and sharp.

Folks say the deputy is watching.

Not just the deputy, he thought. Not anymore.

Charlie Randall left Galeton as the light bled from the sky, unaware that each step away from the town only tightened the web already forming around his name.

Part 2

Austin

9

Arrival in Austin

October 9 (evening), 1898 - Austin

Charlie reached Austin near sundown, his boots dragging through the last mile along a wide, rutted road cut deep by wagons hauling timber for the Goodyear mills. Smoke drifted from the stacks in thick bands, settling low in the valley. It mixed with tannery fumes until the air carried the taste of chemicals and wet bark on the tongue. The town moved with a weary, determined rhythm, the kind that belonged to men who spent more time working than sleeping.

He rented a narrow room above a seamstress's shop, splashed water over his face from a chipped basin, and stepped back outside before the sky fully dimmed. Austin did not quiet at dusk the way smaller towns did. Shift whistles still cried in the distance. Heavy machinery groaned on. Men spilled from alleys and mill yards in loose clusters, shoulders sagging, clothes dark with sweat and resin.

Bark peelers. Sawyers. Doggers. Camp crews just down from the hills. Railroad brakemen stiff from long rides.

They did not head for home. They turned instead toward the places where a dry county bent its own rules.

Charlie followed the flow, letting the streets teach him the town. He watched how men moved, who walked together, who kept apart. Timber camps, rail spurs, towns that grew fast and forgot faster. A man could pass through them without leaving much behind, if he chose his steps carefully.

Austin spread wider than Galeton, buildings pressed close to mill yards and rail lines. Each block opened another seam of the town's underside. Walkways patched too many times. Workers' shacks leaning under their own weight. The faint glow of lanterns hidden behind warped boards.

A narrow alley behind a cooper's shop caught his eye. The mud there lay worn flat by boots, not churned. A door sat tucked beneath a stack of battered barrels, its edges blackened by years of smoke. Men slipped inside one at a time, speaking low, shoulders tight from long shifts.

Charlie followed.

Lanterns hung low inside, their light catching on sawdust drifting from the rafters like weak snowfall. Mill workers crowded a small counter, trading tin cups of illegal whiskey for coins they could not spare. Most wore Goodyear tags stitched to their coats. Some still carried the green smell of sap from the woods.

Charlie stayed near the wall and listened.

Pay was late again.
Crews were being pushed harder.
A rail shipment had gone missing, or perhaps had never arrived.
Company scrip was shrinking, dollar by dollar, week by week.

Men spoke these things without lifting their eyes, as if volume itself might invite notice.

Charlie stayed only long enough to take the measure. No real gambling here. Just quiet anger and tired bodies, and the kind of talk that gathered weight over time.

He slipped back into the street.

Austin's night thickened quickly. Voices rose at the far end of the block where mill hands argued about a foreman's temper. A wagon rattled past bearing stripped hemlock bark, the load swaying with each rut. Railroad lanterns blinked near a siding where crews uncoupled cars for the night.

Charlie followed a pair of bark yard workers who peeled away toward a narrow gap between a laundry and a sagging livery stable. Stone steps dropped behind the building, slick with moss and shadow. The men descended without a word.

Charlie waited a breath, then followed.

The second pig's ear was colder, its stone walls holding the night like damp memory. Dice rattled in a wooden bowl. Two lanterns flickered over the tables, barely cutting the dark. The men here were leaner, harder. River drivers. Bark peelers. A couple of timber cruisers who looked as though they belonged more to the woods than to town.

Charlie took a place near the wall and listened.

"The pay wagon missed last cycle."
"Foreman says it is the books, but the books do not walk off."
"Some stranger was asking questions up the rail spur last week. Did not look like a man who knew a saw."
"Goodyear shorting us again, I reckon."

Voices sharpened when the dice grew tense, but every flare of anger died quickly. Men who hauled timber and fought logjams did not waste breath on shouting unless someone truly earned it.

A saw filer with arms like mill beams ended one argument with a look. The room settled at once.

Charlie stayed long enough to learn something else.

Austin was not simply tired. Austin was unsettled.

He climbed back toward the street, boots scuffing stone, and drew in the heavy night air. Tannery smoke thickened, and beneath it drifted the smell of meat cooking somewhere nearby, rich and immediate.

He followed that scent.

Two streets over he found the restaurant he had heard mentioned twice in passing. A narrow place wedged between warehouses, windows fogged from heat. Men entered in pairs and did not linger in the dining room.

Charlie stepped inside. The woman behind the counter stirred a pot but fixed her eyes on him as he crossed the room. The air smelled of onions, stew, and beneath that, the sharper burn of contraband whiskey.

He passed through a narrow rear doorway into a storage room lined with crates. A boy sorting vegetables kept his eyes down. A weary millman propped in the doorway shifted just enough to let Charlie through, though his gaze lingered a moment longer than necessary.

The kitchen beyond was sweltering. Steam rose from pots. A cook chopped meat without looking up. Two men carried bowls away, not toward tables, but deeper into the building.

Charlie pushed aside the curtain at the far end.

The room beyond burst with sound. Lanterns swung overhead, throwing hard light across card tables packed with mill hands. Woodworkers and tannery men shouted over one another, bets landing as fast as fists. Smoke coiled thick and alive. Whiskey poured from jug to cup without pause.

At the center sat the man Charlie had heard whispered about in both pig's ears.

William Mathewson. Pig's Ear Billy.

A sawmill bruiser turned underground proprietor. Broad shouldered. Knuckles worn smooth by use. Eyes bright with the confidence of a man who ran places like this and answered to no one he could see.

Billy slapped down a winning hand, barked something that carried half laugh and half challenge, then looked up.

Saw Charlie. Measured him slowly.

No smile. No threat. Just interest, sharp and clean.

Charlie gave a slight nod. Billy returned it, barely there.

Charlie eased farther into the room, letting the heat and noise settle over him. This was the true pulse of Austin. A place where Goodyear's labor force spent breath and wages in equal measure. A room where stories moved faster than cards, where a stranger's face could be marked and remembered long before he spoke.

A thin pocket of quiet formed near the doorway as he stepped deeper in. Not silence; Austin never gave that. But a shift, subtle and familiar, the kind that came when men noticed a stranger and had not yet decided what to do with him.

A few players lifted their eyes. Two bark peelers paused mid-sentence. One runner slowed as he passed, giving Charlie the quick, measuring look of a man who remembered faces for a living.

Then the room swelled again. Noise returned as if the moment had been set aside rather than broken. Charlie felt the weight of it settle on him. Not danger yet. But attention, and attention had a way of becoming something else if a man stayed too long or moved too quickly.

He kept his posture loose. His expression calm. He would not sit at a table tonight. Not until he understood the rhythm of the room. The loyalties. The fractures.

He watched. He listened.

Austin moved with a restless hunger that pressed from every side, and Charlie felt it clearly now. Whatever trouble had begun in Galeton had reached this valley ahead of him, even if no one had spoken his name.

10

Pig's Ear Billy

October 10 (night), 1898 - Austin

The next night settled heavy and close, the kind of heat that clung to the back of the throat. One by one the mills groaned themselves quiet, but Austin did not soften with them. It sharpened.

Charlie walked the same streets as before, keeping his pace easy. Men poured out of the yards, faces smeared with dust, shirts plastered to their backs. A few turned toward home. Most did not. They drifted instead toward the same corners, the same alleys, the same doors that swallowed workers and returned them poorer and more tired.

He passed the cooper's cellar and the stone steps behind the laundry without slowing. He knew now where those paths led. Tonight his business lay through the restaurant.

The windows were fogged again. The smell of stew and onions met him at the door, but beneath it ran the sharper scent that truly drew men inside. Whiskey. Sweat. Smoke.

The woman behind the counter glanced at him once, then turned back to her pot. She knew where he was going. So did he.

Charlie crossed the front room, slipped through the storage space, and passed the kitchen where knives knocked against boards and spoons rang against pots. Steam rose thick and wet. The cooks did not look up. Men like Charlie did not cross their floor for supper.

He reached for the curtain at the back.

Before he could lift it, the fabric burst outward.

Two men crashed through, arms tangled, boots skidding in the kitchen slop. One hit the far wall and slid down laughing, his words blurred beyond meaning. The other stumbled, caught himself on a shelf, and reached for a pot as if it might steady him.

A voice followed them.

"Get out of my way."

William Mathewson came through the curtain with the force of a thrown log. He seized the standing drunk by the collar and spun him. The man swung once, wide and slow. Billy caught the blow on his shoulder and answered with a shove that sent the drunk reeling through the doorway and into the front room.

The man struck a table and went down in a crash of crockery.

Billy turned on the second drunk, who sat slumped against the wall, grinning up at him.

"You want to sleep it off in here," Billy asked, "or outside with the garbage."

The man tried to answer and produced a sound that was neither apology nor protest.

Billy hauled him upright as if he weighed nothing and dragged him through the curtain, across the kitchen, and shoved him toward the outer door.

"Go home," Billy said. "Come back when your legs remember how to stand."

The door banged shut.

The cooks returned to their work without comment.

Billy rolled his shoulder once, working out the last echo of the punch, then looked at Charlie.

"You lost," he asked.

"Finding my way," Charlie said.

Billy studied him a moment longer, then lifted the curtain aside with one hand.

"Then come through proper," he said. "Not on your back."

Charlie stepped into the room beyond.

Heat hit first, then sound. The pig's ear throbbed with the same rough energy as the night before, but drawn tighter. Men hovered nearer the edge of their tempers, laughter pitched higher, words sharpened by drink and debt. Wages had been spent. Resentment remained.

Billy moved to the main table and dropped into his chair with the ease of a man reclaiming ground that had never truly been lost.

"You looking to sit," he asked, not bothering to look up.

"If there is a place."

"There is always a place for money," Billy said. "Question is what shape it leaves in."

A few men chuckled. One shifted aside and gestured toward the chair at Billy's right.

Charlie took it.

Cards were already in motion. A small pile of mixed coin and scrip lay in the center. The players were a familiar sort. Two sawmill hands still in their work shirts. A bark peeler with scarred thumbs. A thin man with clean nails who seemed out of place until the Goodyear badge on his coat caught the light.

"New face sits," the thin man said. "Means new luck."

"Luck is not something you borrow," Billy said. "It is something that breaks your nose if you think it owes you."

He nodded to the dealer. The shuffle began.

Charlie watched the cards. Watched hands. Watched how often eyes flicked toward Billy even when he said nothing. Mathewson did not need to raise his voice to own the room. The weight of him did the work.

The first hands ran small. Charlie folded twice, called once, won a modest pot with a pair no one challenged. It gave him time to feel the table's rhythm. Billy played fast and loose, bluffing without shame, retreating without apology. The bark peeler chased losses. The thin man with the badge played tight, jaw flexing each time he laid his cards down.

Between hands, a boy slipped in and leaned close to Billy.

"Message came up from the siding," the boy said softly. "Notes are short again."

Billy's eyes narrowed.

"Short how."

"Two bundles missing off the list. Not scrip. Real paper. Goodyear wants to know where it went."

Billy grunted.

"Goodyear wants to know plenty," he said. "Tell them to start with their own pockets."

The boy swallowed. "They will not like that."

"They will like hearing nothing even less," Billy said. "Go on."

The boy vanished.

Charlie set his cards face down and studied Billy from the corner of his eye. Missing notes. Not scrip this time. Cash. A ripple moved through the room as the news traveled quietly.

One of the sawmill hands could not leave it alone.

"You think someone here is lifting it," he asked. "Or is this another one of those bookkeeping tricks."

Billy turned his head slowly.

"You accusing me of something."

The man swallowed. "No. Just saying someone ought to answer if we are being shorted again."

"Maybe someone will," Billy said. "But it will not be over table talk."

Silence moved around the table like a draft. The next hand was dealt without comment.

Charlie picked up his cards. Middling. Enough to stay, not enough to push. He played it through for the talk more than the pot.

Across from him, the thin man with the badge could not keep his eyes from Billy.

"You are sure nothing went missing here," he asked carefully. "Nothing moved through your room that should not have."

Billy laid his cards down untouched.

"This room keeps its own book," he said. "And its owner remembers every line. You want to tell your employers they dropped something, do it. But do not sit in my chair and hint I have sticky fingers."

The man flushed. "I did not say that."

"You did not have to," Billy replied. "You thought it."

The bark peeler laughed once, too loud.

Billy did not look at him. His eyes stayed on the company man until the fellow picked up his cards again and stared at them like they might offer escape.

Charlie folded early. Distance, even symbolic, mattered. The pot slid to Billy, who barely acknowledged it.

Another boy slipped through with a folded note. Billy read it, snorted, and crumpled the paper.

"Missing here, missing there," he muttered. "Whole valley is nothing but holes in a bucket."

He snapped his fingers at the thin man.

"Tell your bosses this. I did not take their notes. I do not need their scraps. This room pays its own way."

"They will want more than that," the man said.

Billy met his eyes.

"Then they can come ask me themselves," he said. "See how long their boots stay clean."

The man looked away.

The game continued, but the tone had shifted. Laughter cut sharper. Men drank faster. Bets crept higher.

Charlie adjusted his play. Two small wins. One loss. Nothing loud. Each time he gathered his chips, he felt eyes on his hands. Billy's most of all.

Between hands, Billy spoke without turning.

"You from the Goodyear side," he asked, "or somewhere else."

"Just passing through," Charlie said. "Looking for work that does not involve lifting things I cannot put back."

"Cards, then."

"Cards."

"Men who say that usually bring trouble," Billy said. "Sometimes the kind worth having."

"And sometimes not," Charlie said.

Billy's mouth curved thinly. "I prefer trouble I can see coming."

"I do not hide my hands."

Billy studied him fully now.

"No," he said. "That might be what worries me."

He flicked a card across the felt toward Charlie, more test than deal.

"Sit as long as you like," Billy said. "Win if you can. Lose if that is the night's choice. Just remember this. I do not mind a man taking money from my table, so long as he is only playing cards."

"And if he is not."

"Then he is playing something else," Billy said. "And I want to know who taught him the rules."

The next hand began.

Charlie picked up his cards, the weight of the words settling between them. Missing notes. Company nerves. Billy's temper held tight, but only just.

Charlie played the rest of the night carefully. Modest gains. Quiet retreats. When his stack grew enough to draw notice, he stood.

"You leaving early," Billy asked.

"Early keeps a man in one piece."

Billy nodded. "Come back tomorrow if you are still in town. I like knowing what kind of trouble sits at my right."

Charlie inclined his head and stepped away.

He passed back through the kitchen heat, through the storage room, and into the cooler air of the front.

Austin remained awake. Laughter carried too far. Someone argued near the rail spur. A dog barked without much conviction.

Charlie walked toward his narrow room, hands in his pockets, thoughts turning.

Billy had not accused him.

Not yet.

But the pig's ear kept its own ledger, and tonight Charlie had been entered into it.

In a town where money and missing notes were beginning to pull against each other, a gambler with a steady hand and a quiet name would not remain unnoticed for long.

11

A Familiar Scrip

October 11, 1898 - Austin

Charlie woke later than usual, the room already warm with trapped air and the tannery smell creeping through the open window. Austin never truly quieted, not even at night, and the clatter of shifting freight and late-shift mill crews still rang faintly in his bones. He lay still for a moment, letting the noise settle into something he could ignore.

He stepped outside with the morning crowd, coat collar turned up against the damp chill that lingered in the shade. Sunlight cut long stripes across the muddy road. The mills were already groaning, saws biting into timber, belts slapping and humming. Fine dust drifted from open windows like pale ash. Men moved with the tired precision of those who did not expect rest to come easily.

Charlie walked without hurry, letting the town speak for itself. Austin was broader than Galeton, louder and more crowded, built tight around industry instead of forest. The air tasted of tannins and steam. The ground trembled when heavy logs rolled along chains.

He passed the freight spur and the bark yards, then paused near the riverbank where men sorted through wet piles of bark, hands stained dark from tannery work. Nothing here felt gentle. Even the wind seemed to scrape at a man.

By midday he had learned enough to feel the town's rhythm. Hard work. Hard drink. Hard secrets.

He returned to the house where he rented his room. Mrs. Albright stood on the porch, sweeping the steps with short, efficient strokes. She was thin and straight-backed, a kerchief tied tight over her hair.

"You were in late last night," she said without looking up.

"Lost track of time," Charlie replied.

She swept another line across the step. "Men who lose track of time in Austin usually lose more than that. Watch yourself."

Charlie nodded. Advice like that was rarely offered without cause.

Inside, he hung his coat and sat for a time, listening to the steady pulse of the mills through the walls. Weariness caught up with him all at once. He lay back on the narrow bed and let the noise blur. Sleep took him quickly and held him deep.

* * *

He woke before dawn. Cool air slid through the window and cleared the room of the previous day's heaviness. He washed, dressed, and stepped into the street while the lamps still burned weak and yellow.

Breakfast came from a kettle near the boarding houses, a ladle of porridge served by a woman whose voice barely carried. Charlie ate slowly, watching the sky pale behind the mill roofs.

He walked the edge of the Goodyear works next, taking in the long sheds and the machinery that never seemed to rest. Workers hauled fresh cut logs from wagons, boots sinking into ground softened by years of sawdust. Steam hissed from pipes near the tannery and drifted low across the yard like morning fog.

Nothing here felt careless. Nothing felt accidental either. Austin ran on labor and pressure, and both were stretched tight.

When the sun climbed higher, Charlie made his way toward town.

The post office stood quiet when he reached it. The line was short. The postmaster, a heavy man with a neat mustache, sorted envelopes while talking freely to anyone nearby.

"The Goodyear pay wagon was late again," he said to a railroad man. "Never had this much trouble before this year."

"Trouble how," Charlie asked when his turn came.

The postmaster tipped his head, studying him. "You are new here."

"Passing through."

The man accepted that and lowered his voice. "Workers say their pay is short or delayed. Company blames schedules. Maybe that is true. Maybe not. Happens when money starts moving faster than men can count."

Charlie thanked him and stepped aside. Outside, he walked slowly, turning the words over.

Missing scrip or miscounted.
Late wagons.
Men growing restless.

He had heard that tune before, north in Galeton, wrapped in rumor and unease. The same notes now rang through Austin.

He spent the afternoon listening. Mill hands complained of long hours. Bark peelers muttered about fights in the lower ward. A brakeman swore someone had been lifting tools from the night shift. Each story carried the same undercurrent. Pressure building. Money thinning. Tempers stretched close to breaking.

By dusk, the weight of the day sat heavy behind his ribs. Charlie returned to Mrs. Albright's long enough to wash the grit from his hands and collar. When the street lamps flickered to life, he stepped back out.

The restaurant that hid Billy's pig's ear was crowded tonight. Men packed the front tables, eating fast or lifting mugs that smelled nothing like anything the law allowed. Charlie moved through them without drawing notice, slipped past the heat of the kitchen, and followed the narrow corridor into the back.

Lantern light washed over the room. Smoke thickened the air. Voices collided in rough conversation. Billy sat in his usual place, boots set wide, a sliver of toothpick shifting between his teeth as he watched the tables.

Charlie took a seat at a smaller game along the side wall, easing himself into the night's rhythm.

The cards ran slow at first. Modest pots. A few easy laughs. The comfort of routine.

Then the man across from him slid a clean stack of scrip into the center of the table.

Charlie knew it before he read the date.

Goodyear scrip. Future dated. The same kind that had changed the air in Galeton.

He felt the recognition tighten behind his eyes. He kept his breathing even and tapped the corner of his cards against the table.

"Picked it up from a runner," the man said casually. "Came down the rail spur today. Said he was clearing accounts early."

The bark peeler beside him nodded.

Charlie folded without hesitation. The cards disappeared into the discard pile.

The man who had laid down the scrip gathered the pot and said, almost to himself, "If that ledger ever turns up, they will shut the yards for a month sorting it out."

"Or longer," the bark peeler muttered. "Depends whose names are in it."

"Names don't matter," a third voice said quietly. "Numbers do. You show men they been shorted for years, they will burn a place down just to feel square again."

Around him, the room carried on, loud with drink and bravado. No one else cared about the paper in that pot. No one questioned the date, the source, or why runners were moving money before the company called for it.

Charlie leaned back, letting the haze settle around him.

This was no coincidence. The same quiet confidence wrapped in future scrip had crossed his path twice now. Someone was moving paper through these towns with pattern and intent.

The thread that had brushed him in Galeton had reached Austin as well. Or perhaps he had been walking along it longer than he knew.

Either way, its shape was coming into focus.

And the center of it lay closer than he liked to admit.

12

Eli Mahon's Warning

October 11 (night), 1898 - Austin

The pig's ear was working toward a boil. Lanterns hung low from iron hooks, their light thickening the smoke until faces blurred at the edges. Heat leaked through the back wall from the kitchen, mixing with sweat and the sour bite of illegal liquor passed hand to hand in chipped mugs.

Charlie had been sitting at the edge table for nearly an hour. He played little, won less, and watched constantly. One eye tracked the door. The other followed the runners who slipped through the room with the practiced ease of men who carried more than messages.

Charlie never chose a table by the cards. He chose it by the men.

A loud table meant mistakes. A quiet one meant discipline. What he wanted was something in between. Men willing to talk, but not willing to lose. That was where the money lasted long enough to be taken.

That was when Eli Mahon came in.

Eli could have been sixteen, maybe seventeen. Narrow shoulders. Quick eyes. Feet that never seemed to rest. His cap sat too large on his head, and his coat hung wrong, one sleeve torn at the seam. Runners in Austin often looked like that. Half-fed. Always listening.

Charlie had noticed him the night before, hovering near Billy's table, delivering folded scraps of paper to men who pretended not to see him.

Tonight, Eli kept to the wall. He stayed in the darker seams of the room, scanning faces with the anxious precision of someone waiting for a moment that might not come. When his eyes crossed Charlie's, he froze, then looked away too quickly.

Charlie kept his gaze on his cards. He let the boy come to him or not at all.

Two hands passed. Then three.

The room tightened as more men crowded in from the late shift. Boots thudded on the floorboards. Someone near the bar began shouting about miscounted scrip. Billy half rose from his chair, then settled back when the argument burned itself out without needing him.

Eli drifted closer. Not straight in. Not enough to draw notice. He angled his way behind Charlie's chair and stopped, pretending to watch the game.

Charlie did not look up. "You looking for someone," he asked quietly.

Eli flinched. "Keep your voice down."

He glanced toward Billy's table, then toward the door, measuring both before speaking again.

When Charlie gathered his small winnings and pushed back his chair, Eli edged toward the narrow corridor leading to the kitchen. Charlie followed at an easy pace, neither hurrying nor hanging back.

Near the end of the hallway, Eli stopped beside a stack of crates half lost in shadow. Steam drifted along the ceiling from the kitchen beyond. He spoke without lifting his eyes.

"You need to leave Austin."

Charlie folded his arms loosely. "That so. Why."

Eli swallowed. "Because people already think you are part of something. Something you are not supposed to be part of."

Charlie watched him carefully. "What do they think I am part of."

The boy hesitated, eyes fixed on Charlie's boots. "Missing scrip. Pay notes gone before they reach the hands meant for them." His voice dropped lower. "Someone said your name when it started."

The words settled hard.

Charlie let the silence stretch, long enough to see if Eli would fill it.

Eli did.

"Men do not ask questions about scrip disappearing," he said. "They only look for someone to blame. And they think you know where it went."

"I do not," Charlie said.

"That never mattered," Eli replied. He finally looked up. His eyes were sharp, but there was fear behind them now. "They already drew the lines. You walked into them without knowing."

Charlie studied him for a long moment, weighing the boy as he would a table. "Who told you to warn me."

"No one," Eli said quickly. He wiped his palms on his coat. "Someone helped me once. Back in Galeton. I owed something. This settles it."

Charlie's attention sharpened. "Who helped you."

Eli's mouth tightened. He glanced toward the wall, as if he expected someone to be listening from inside it.

"Look, men don't want that book found," he said. "Not because of money. Money can be settled."

Charlie waited, saying nothing.

"Men don't get ruined by what's written in that book," Eli said. "They get ruined by who decides what gets counted." He shook his head once, as if the thought itself carried weight. "It is the kind of thing that makes people disappear. The kind that gets blamed on rivers or trains or bad luck."

The corridor felt narrower with the words in it.

Eli drew a breath, steadying himself. "I said what I came to say. Leave Austin before nightfall tomorrow. And if anyone asks, you did not hear it from me."

Charlie held him there a moment longer. "You are certain they said my name."

Eli nodded once. "Certain enough."

Then he slipped past Charlie and vanished into the steam of the kitchen, moving with the speed of someone who had already stayed too long.

Charlie stood alone in the narrow corridor, listening to the roar of the room on the other side of the wall. Boots on boards. Voices rising and falling. The steady churn of a place that did not stop long enough to notice what it was becoming.

His name had reached Austin ahead of him. Not as a gambler. Not as a stranger passing through. As something else. Something useful.

He had seen it before. Not the same place. Not the same men. But the pattern was familiar enough. A name spoken in the wrong room. Repeated once too often. Then carried where it did not belong.

Someone had written him into a story he did not recognize, and that story was already moving without him.

He stepped back into the pig's ear and let the door fall shut behind him. The room swallowed him again, loud and restless, thick with heat and drink. But the night no longer felt like a place for cards.

It felt like a notice. And notices, in towns like this, were never issued without intent.

13

Billy's Suspicion

October 12 (night), 1898 - Austin

The next night came on heavy, as if the heat from the mills had sunk into the streets and refused to lift. Charlie walked toward the restaurant slowly, keeping to the edges of the road, watching the gaps between buildings where shadows gathered and held. Eli's warning had rested in his mind all day like a stone dropped into water, sending quiet ripples through every thought.

He had considered leaving Austin before dawn. He had even packed his things.

But leaving without understanding the shape of the trouble felt too much like running blind. And running blind had never saved any man he knew.

So he walked back toward the pig's ear, not for cards, but for answers.

Inside the restaurant, the dinner rush had thinned. Grease clung to the air. A tired cook scraped pans in the kitchen, the sound sharp and final. Charlie threaded through the heat and noise and down the narrow corridor to the back room.

The pig's ear was already full.

Tonight the room carried a different strain. Laughter came short and forced. Conversations stopped when certain men passed too close. A few runners lingered near the door like birds ready to scatter at the first sharp sound.

Billy sat in his usual place, but his posture had hardened. His elbows rested wide on the table, shoulders tight beneath his shirt. He looked up the moment Charlie stepped inside.

Charlie kept his movements slow and ordinary. He took an open seat near the wall and nodded to the men already there.

No one nodded back.

The cards began to move. Charlie played small, careful hands, folding early, winning nothing worth remark. Still, each time he reached for the pot, he felt Billy's attention tighten across the room like a drawn wire.

Two more hands passed.

Then the noise thinned.

Billy stood.

He did not announce himself. He simply moved through the room, slow and solid, weaving between tables until he stopped beside Charlie's chair. His shadow spilled across the felt.

"You walk in here again," Billy said quietly, "and I still do not know who put wind in your sails."

Charlie did not look up. "I came to play a few hands."

"That would be a comfort," Billy said, "if I believed you came here for cards."

The room leaned without leaning. Men found reasons to pause. Charlie folded his hand and set it aside.

"I do not want trouble," he said.

"No," Billy replied. "But trouble seems to want you."

Billy studied him, eyes searching for something beneath the calm. Fear. Guilt. Or the shape of a lie practiced too well.

"I hear you been asking questions," Billy said. "I hear you been studying scrip like it might speak back. I hear you came down from up north where a man your size and name already stirred things loose."

Charlie's voice stayed even. "Rumors travel faster than truth."

Billy's mouth twitched. "They do. And what matters in a room like this is not where a rumor starts. It is where it decides to sit."

Charlie said nothing.

Billy tapped a knuckle against the table, once. The sound cut clean through the air.

"Men come in here and win," Billy said. "Men lose too. But they all stand on something solid. Then there is you."

He leaned closer. "You arrive quiet. You watch more than you play. You win just enough to stay noticed. And the same week missing notes start getting named, you are sitting in my room."

"I had nothing to do with that," Charlie said.

Billy straightened and rolled his shoulders once. "Maybe. Or maybe you do not yet understand what you brushed up against."

He tilted his chin toward the corridor. "Here is how tonight goes. You keep your head down. You play clean. And when I say you walk, you walk. But if you stir dust again, I will sweep it out myself."

The room held still. Lanterns hissed softly. A chair creaked as someone shifted their weight.

Charlie nodded once. "I understand."

"Good," Billy said, though his tone carried no relief. "Because this town has very little patience left. And patience, once spent, does not come back."

He stepped away but kept his eyes on Charlie for a moment longer, as if fixing his measure.

Then Billy returned to his chair, and the room eased back into motion, conversation restarting in cautious fragments.

Charlie watched the next hand being dealt but did not reach for his cards. He listened instead. To the soft rasp of scrip changing hands. To the clipped exchanges near the wall. To the silence that settled whenever someone glanced his way.

Eli had been right. Something had already chosen him as its pivot.

And Billy, for all his confidence, could feel it circling too.

Charlie pushed back from the table.

He did not announce himself. He nodded once to the dealer and stepped toward the corridor.

No one stopped him. But the eyes that followed him out were colder than when he had come in.

Outside, the night air cut sharper than expected.

Whatever had begun in Galeton had fully arrived in Austin. Whatever shape it took next would not wait long.

Billy's suspicion was not the cause.

It was the signal.

The sign that the ground beneath Charlie's feet had already begun to shift.

14

Rumors of a Dead Man

October 13 (night), 1898 - Austin

Charlie stayed clear of Billy's pig's ear the next night. Going back there felt like stepping willingly into a snare already half drawn. Instead, he walked Austin's darker back streets until he found another place where liquor passed hand to hand and talk loosened with it.

The second pig's ear sat behind a shuttered cobbler's shop near the river. The door bore no sign, only a lantern hung low enough to look accidental. A man outside gave Charlie a measured look, tapped a short rhythm against his boot heel, and the door eased open from within.

Inside, the room was smaller and older than Billy's, its walls darkened by years of smoke. Lanterns hung at uneven heights, throwing light that made faces look half finished. The men gathered here were older too. Bark peelers, river drivers, sawyers whose hands had stiffened with age and weather. They drank slow, played slow, and spoke as if each word cost something.

Charlie took a seat against the wall. The best way to learn anything in a town like Austin was to let its men forget you were listening.

A game of Thirty-One played out at the nearest table. Cards snapped. Coins slid. Voices rose and fell with the weight of long familiarity.

Then, mid-hand, an older logger leaned back and said, "You hear that business again. Ebenspecker. Came up this afternoon near the bark piles."

The younger man beside him shook his head. “That was three years ago.”

“Eighteen ninety-five,” the older one said. “Feels closer than that to men who knew him.”

Charlie did not move, but every sense sharpened.

The younger man frowned. “Thought he drowned.”

“That’s what the constable said,” the older logger replied. “Said George got drunk and stumbled into the creek in Blowville. Printed it that way too. Folks let it sit.”

Another man snorted softly into his drink. “A man does not split the back of his head open on creek water.”

The table quieted, not sudden, but careful.

The older logger nodded once. “That was the part nobody spoke loud. Not in Blowville. Not in Costello. They found him facedown in the shallows behind the north footbridge. Clothes soaked. Boots still laced. But the back of his skull was opened. Men who saw him said no fall did that.”

A third man leaned in, voice lowered. “He saw something he was not meant to see. That much I always believed.”

The younger man scraped a coin across the table. “What would a man like that see.”

“Scrip,” the older one said. “Or the way it moved. George hauled bark when Blowville needed extra hands. Went where Fee sent him. If he stumbled onto ledgers or runners or payouts that did not line up, he would have asked why. And some men do not like that question.”

The cards lay untouched now.

“George wasn’t the first,” one of the older men said. “Just the one folks remember.”

“Remember for what,” another asked.

The man shrugged. “For asking why some men got paid clean and others got told to wait. For wondering how the books always balanced when the hands never did.”

Someone snorted softly. “If a ledger ever kept those answers straight, no one would dare open it now.”

Charlie kept his breathing even.

Another man spoke, quieter still. “I heard Crane killed him.”

The reaction was immediate. Not outrage. Not defense. Something tighter.

The older logger answered at once. “Crane did not kill him. Odd fellow, yes. But he did not run after George died. Stayed in Blowville. Took his shifts. Walked like a man carrying old weight, but he never bolted.”

“So who did it,” the younger man asked.

The older logger blew out a slow breath. “Could have been runners tied to the Goodyear line. Could have been someone settled between Austin and Costello. Could have been someone in Blowville who needed a dead man to look like an accident.”

He paused.

“But Crane,” he added, “knew how things were written. That much was plain. He knew where names went, and where they did not. After George died, the books stayed clean. Too clean.”

The younger man nodded grimly. “Company printed the accident story quick. Too quick.”

“That is how you keep a town quiet,” the older one said. “Give them a simple death instead of a complicated truth.”

The talk thinned after that, easing back into cards and drink. But the name lingered in the air like smoke that refused to lift.

George Ebenspecker.
Blowville.
The creek.
The wound no one was meant to see.

And Crane, not accused, not chased, but present all the same. A man whose name never appeared where it should have, and whose absence from blame felt deliberate.

Charlie rose after a time and stepped back outside. The night smelled of river mud and tannery smoke, heavy enough to coat the tongue.

He walked slowly, letting the pieces settle.

George had died in Blowville. Not from drink, but from something deliberate. Crane had not vanished afterward. He had stayed. Which meant whoever was responsible had not feared him, or had trusted his silence.

That truth aligned too neatly with the stolen scrip. The future dates. The quiet movement of money no one was meant to notice.

The ledger Charlie had never seen, but could now feel the weight of all the same.

George's death had not closed a chapter. It had opened one. A first crack running through years of careful quiet.

And now Charlie had stepped into the same fracture, without knowing who had pushed him or why.

He walked on as the night closed in behind him. The trouble that had begun in Galeton was no longer distant.

It had roots in Blowville.

And it had started long before Charlie ever knew his name would be spoken aloud.

15

Ambushed

October 13 (late night), 1898 - Austin

Charlie left the second pig's ear with the sense that the night had given him all it intended to. The talk of George Ebenspecker clung to him, settling beside Eli's warning and the quiet pressure that had begun to follow him through Austin like a second presence.

The streets lay mostly empty. The mills had gone quiet, but they still breathed heat into the alleys. Lanterns glowed weakly behind greasy windows. Somewhere a dog barked once and then fell silent, as if corrected.

Charlie kept to the side streets, moving with the same measured caution he carried into card rooms. He had learned long ago that danger favored the margins of towns, the places where sound thinned and light failed.

He passed the freight spur and crossed a narrow footbridge over a drainage ditch. Ahead, the road curved behind a tannery storage building. Smoke from the vats drifted low across the path, turning lantern light into a trembling haze that swallowed distance.

He took two steps into the smoke before he heard it.

A scuff of boots. Too close. More than one.

Charlie stopped, but the pause came too late.

Figures stepped out of the fog like shapes lifting from river water. Three of them, maybe four. The steam made counting difficult. Faces were hidden behind scarves. Jackets pulled tight. Men dressed to vanish.

The tallest spoke first. “Evening, Randall.”

Charlie felt his pulse tighten. No one in Austin should have known his name.

He did not step back. He did not reach for anything. Sudden movement invited decisions he could not afford.

“What do you want,” he asked.

A man to his right lifted a short club wrapped in cloth. “The ledger.”

Charlie said nothing.

The tall man took a step forward. “You know which one. You came into Austin asking questions. Looking at scrip too close. That tells us you saw something. Or someone handed you something you were not meant to have.”

“I have no ledger,” Charlie said.

The tall man’s voice stayed level, almost patient. “You are going to give it over. Or you are going to bleed until someone finds it on you.”

Another man shifted behind Charlie, cutting off the way back toward the bridge.

Charlie kept his breathing slow. “You have the wrong man.”

“Funny,” the tall one said. “That is what men usually say right before they change their minds.”

The man with the club stepped closer, swinging it once in a lazy arc, testing the space. Charlie shifted his weight just enough to mark where he would go if the first blow came.

The smoke thickened, heavy with chemicals and boiled bark. A lantern flickered above the tannery door, throwing light just far enough to show the glint of another club.

“Last chance,” the tall man said.

Charlie did not answer. The silence unsettled them. He felt it in the tightening of shoulders, the way one man leaned too far forward.

The club came down.

Charlie twisted aside. The blow struck the wall with a dull thud that shuddered through the stone. A hand grabbed at his coat. He tore free, ducking low, but another figure filled the gap, swinging hard. The strike caught him across the shoulder, pain burning down his arm.

He staggered but stayed on his feet.

Another blow came from the left. He dodged, felt it scrape his ribs, and knew he could not absorb many more.

He drove forward without warning, slamming his shoulder into the smallest man. The impact knocked the breath from him and sent him crashing back into the others. For a heartbeat their footing tangled.

It was enough.

Charlie slipped past the wall and plunged into the thickest part of the smoke.

Shouts followed.
"There."
"Behind the vats."
"Get him."

He ran blind, trusting the ground more than his eyes. Steam stung his face. Heat pressed close. Boots closed in behind him. He heard the scrape of wood on stone as someone recovered a dropped club.

A narrow alley opened on his right. Charlie cut into it, boots sliding on wet cobblestones, and pressed his back to the wall. The men rushed past the alley's mouth, swallowed by smoke and momentum.

For a moment, the night went still.

Charlie eased along the wall, moving deeper into the alley until he reached the far end. He climbed over a short stack of crates, dropped quietly on the other side, and crouched beneath a loading platform. His shoulder throbbed. His breath came shallow, careful.

Voices drifted nearby, confused and angry, spreading toward the river road.

Charlie waited until they faded.

He did not feel safe. He did not feel finished. But he had a narrow pocket of silence to think.

Someone knew his name.
Someone believed he carried a ledger he had never seen.
Someone was ready to beat answers out of him.

He stayed crouched until the night cooled against his sweat.

Then he slipped out from beneath the platform and followed the tightest roads back toward town, keeping to shadow, knowing this was only the beginning.

The men who had attacked him had not done so by mistake.

They were hunting something.

And for reasons he did not yet understand, they were certain he had it.

16

Crane's Name Surfaces

October 14, 1898 - Austin

Charlie spent most of the morning moving slowly through Austin, the stiffness from the ambush still clinging to his shoulder. Each step reminded him of the club that had found its mark the night before. Each street reminded him that someone in this town knew his name, his outline, and a lie about a ledger he was supposed to be carrying.

He kept his coat pulled tight, not against the weather but against the looks that lingered a moment too long.

By midmorning the mills were in full roar. Steam hissed from tannery pipes. Wagons rattled over the main road. The smell of bark, sweat, and iron lay so thick in the air it felt like something a man could choke on if he breathed too deeply.

Charlie drifted toward the yards where workers gathered during short breaks. He was not looking for trouble. He was listening for it.

What he heard first were the familiar complaints.

"Pay came light again."
"They say the tallies were off at the spur."
"Company better sort its numbers before winter."

But it was the way men spoke around certain names that caught him. Voices lowered. Eyes cut sideways. Words slowed, as if being weighed before release.

Charlie lingered, adjusting his boot lace, letting the talk find him.

A bark peeler with a bandaged thumb leaned against a stack of stripped bark and said quietly, "Saw Crane down in Blowville last fall. Man never blinked. Always looked like he was listening to something behind you instead of what you were saying."

Charlie kept his head down.

The man beside him scoffed. "Crane. That the fellow works under Terrence Fee. Heard he keeps to himself."

"That is the one," the bark peeler said. "Strange sort."

"Strange how."

"Strange enough," the man replied. "Fee trusts him though. Sends him to Austin sometimes. Sends him up to Costello. Always quiet. Always watching."

Charlie felt a faint chill that had nothing to do with the morning air.

Crane. The same name he had heard whispered in the pig's ear behind the cobbler's shop. The same name that had hovered near George Ebenspecker's death without settling long enough to be blamed.

When the break ended and the men drifted back toward the mills, Charlie moved on. He followed the side road that curved toward the river, where children skipped stones and chased one another between the posts of a half-collapsed fence.

Near the bank, two railroad men crouched beside a toolbox, sharing a cigarette.

"...Crane was asking questions again," one muttered.

The other shook his head. "Man ought to mind his business. Fee is still fit enough to sign orders, but his head is not what it was. If Crane keeps sniffing around the wrong corners, someone is going to clean him up."

Charlie slowed, careful not to look as though he were listening.

"Besides," the first man went on, "folks say Crane been using another name now and then. Makes it hard to keep track of which is which."

“What name.”

“Do not know. Someone from up north.”

Charlie felt his stomach tighten.

The words sank in with a dull weight. The conversation broke apart as a cart rattled past, and the men turned their attention elsewhere.

A name. Passed through these towns like a borrowed tool. Used. Set down. Picked up again when needed.

Charlie walked on until the river widened and the noise of the mills softened behind him. He stood watching the dark water push past the pilings, steady and indifferent. The bruise along his shoulder pulsed in time with his breath.

Crane.

He could not yet put a face to the name. Only an outline. A presence that moved between towns, watching, listening, stepping into places where other men hesitated.

And somewhere along the line, that presence had reached into Charlie’s life. Had taken his name and set it loose among men already looking for someone to blame.

By late afternoon he found himself back near the edge of town. Runners darted between alleys, folded notes passing into hands that should not have been waiting for them. Workers moved with heads down. No one spoke more than necessary.

The pattern sharpened.

Crane had been moving through Austin long before Charlie arrived.
Crane had been brushing the edges of the scrip trade, careful and quiet, while Fee’s authority thinned.
Crane had needed another name.
A name without roots in Blowville.
A name no one would question if trouble followed it.

Charlie Randall, wandering gambler, had been close at hand.

Charlie stood very still.

He did not know Crane. But Crane knew of him. Knew his name well enough to use it. Knew enough to leave him carrying the weight of a ledger that did not exist.

The realization settled cold and deliberate.

He had not walked into another man's trouble. Another man had walked into his life and placed the trouble there on purpose.

As the sun dropped behind the roofs and the mill whistles echoed across the valley, Charlie turned back toward the road leading to his room.

Whatever Crane had begun, it was still unfolding. And whether Charlie wanted it or not, he had already been written into the story.

He needed to know why.

And he needed to know soon.

Before the next voice in the smoke spoke his name aloud.

17

Billy Loses Patience

October 15 (night), 1898 - Austin

Charlie waited another full day before returning to the pig's ear behind the restaurant. He spent the hours walking Austin's alleys and side streets, doubling back when a route felt wrong, testing reflections in darkened windows, listening for more talk of Crane or the movement of stolen scrip. But Austin offered nothing clean. Only smoke, noise, and the persistent sense of being watched by eyes he could not fix in place.

By dusk he understood what avoiding Billy was doing. It was not easing suspicion. It was sharpening it.

So he stepped back through the restaurant kitchen, where steam rolled in heavy waves from boiling pots, and into the narrow corridor that led to the back room.

The pig's ear was busier than he expected. Too busy for a midweek night.

Men crowded the tables shoulder to shoulder. Tempers rode high. Laughter came sharp and brief, as if no one trusted it to linger. The air thrummed with unspent energy that had nowhere to go.

Billy sat at his usual place near the center, elbows wide, shoulders tight, his eyes fixed on the room like weights holding it down. When he saw Charlie, he did not look away. The stare held steady, measuring, the way a man measures distance before acting.

Charlie kept his posture loose as he approached a smaller table near the wall.

He had barely taken his seat before Billy stood.

The room did not fall silent, but it shifted. Cards slowed. Voices dipped. Even the lanterns seemed to hum lower as Billy threaded his way between tables. The crowd parted without a word, bodies moving aside as if pulled by gravity.

Billy stopped beside Charlie, boots planted wide.

"Back again," he said.

Charlie met his gaze. "Just looking to play a clean hand."

Billy leaned forward slightly. "Clean hand. That is what you said last time. Yet the minute you walk out, men start whispering."

"I have not said a word," Charlie replied.

"I know," Billy said. "That is what makes it worse. Quiet men can be useful. They can also be dangerous when they wander where they should not."

Charlie let the silence sit.

Billy tapped the table once with his knuckles. The sound carried farther than it should have. "Two nights now I have heard your name from men who do not know you. Men from the spur. Men from the tannery. Men who claim you brought questions with you."

"Questions about what," Charlie asked.

Billy shook his head slowly. "That is exactly the problem."

A runner drifted up behind Billy, pale and uneasy, hands tucked inside his coat sleeves. "Billy," he said, barely above a whisper. "Heard some talk from the yard. Same name again."

Billy did not turn. "Say it."

"Randall."

The ripple moved through the room this time. Small, but undeniable.

Billy's jaw set. "You see what you have stirred."

"I did not stir anything," Charlie said.

Billy's expression hardened. "Then trouble is following you. Which amounts to the same thing."

He rested one hand on the back of Charlie's chair. Not gripping it. Just resting. The kind of contact that carried weight without force.

"I give leeway to men who work," Billy said. "And I give leeway to men who win or lose with decency. But I do not give leeway to men who drag heat into my hall. Not without cause."

"I did not bring heat here," Charlie said quietly. "Someone else brought my name."

Billy's eyes narrowed. "Then you find out who. Because I will not have the law sniffing around my door on account of a stranger no one stands for."

"I do not plan on bringing the law," Charlie said.

Billy's voice dropped. "You think I care about stolen scrip. Boys steal scrip every week."

He leaned closer. "What I care about is a book that tells the wrong man he was cheated, or tells the law who signed what when they should not have."

He straightened. "That kind of thing does not end in repayment. It ends in indictments or graves. Sometimes both."

Billy spoke up so the whole room could hear. "You have tonight. Play if you want. Watch if you want. But after tonight, you stay out of my rooms until you can look me square and tell me why men keep tying your name to trouble."

"And if I cannot," Charlie asked.

Billy leaned in close enough that only Charlie could hear him. "Then you leave Austin. The soft way or the hard way. That part is up to you."

He straightened, dismissed Charlie with a tilt of his head, and walked back toward his table.

The room began to move again, slowly, like water settling after a stone is dropped.

Charlie let his hands rest on the table. They looked steady enough.

Inside, tension gathered and pulled tight, like a wire drawn too close to breaking.

Everywhere he turned, the same pattern repeated. The same name passed mouth to mouth. The same suspicion. The same shadow cast by a man he had never seen.

Crane.

When the cards came around again, Charlie did not reach for them. His attention stayed on the door, on the runners, on the men who leaned too close and watched too long.

Billy had lost patience.

And when a man like Billy lost patience, the room followed.

Charlie rose, nodded once to the dealer, and stepped toward the corridor. No one stopped him. But more than one man watched him leave.

Outside, the night felt closer than before, the air pressing in as if Austin itself were closing ranks.

If he stayed much longer, someone would make sure he did not walk out whole.

Which meant he needed answers.

Or he needed distance.

Either way, Austin was nearly finished with him.

18

The Web Tightens

October 15, 1898 - Austin

Charlie left Billy's pig's ear with the sense of a noose tightening one knot at a time. The night air lay thick with tannery smoke, drifting low over Austin like a warning that never quite blew away. Men moved through it in quick silhouettes. Voices carried unevenly. Every footstep behind him felt a shade too close.

He did not go straight back to Mrs. Albright's. A man who had just been warned by someone like Billy did not walk the same streets in the same order.

Instead he took the long way along the spur line, where railcars sat stacked with bark bundles and, beneath them, with rumor. Woodsmen huddled near cookfires behind the yards, passing tin cups back and forth. Some nodded to him without warmth. Others watched with that narrow attention that said a man was being measured for danger.

Twice he heard it again.
Randall.
Spoken low, as if the name itself carried weight.

Charlie kept moving, slow enough to look like any other drifter with a long night behind him, quick enough that no one could corner him. He felt the town's attention slide along his back like a hand testing a blade.

When he finally reached his rented room, Mrs. Albright was blowing out the hallway lamp.

"You're out late again," she said. There was no judgment in it, only notice.

"Could not sleep," Charlie answered.

"You won't," she said, tightening the scarf around her shoulders, "if you mix with the wrong circles. Austin has a way of turning strangers into stories. Better to keep yours short."

He thanked her, stepped inside, and bolted the door.

Sleep did not come. Each time he closed his eyes he saw Billy's stare, the quick exchange between runner and room, the stiffness in men's shoulders whenever Crane's name surfaced. Somewhere in Austin, someone knew exactly why Charlie Randall's name had been stitched into this trouble. He simply had not crossed paths with that person yet.

He kept a lantern lit until dawn, listening for footsteps.

None came.

The next afternoon he walked the tannery road again, hoping distance might thin the pressure. Rain threatened overhead. The smell of chemicals mixed with wet bark turned the air sour. Crews hammered planks, stacked hides, shouted over the grind of machinery. A foreman barked at two boys hauling buckets, then held Charlie in his gaze just long enough to suggest he should keep moving.

No welcome anywhere. No direct threat either. Only the steady sense that Austin wanted him gone.

Near dusk he slipped back toward the restaurant, following the alley behind the kitchens. Steam poured from vents and drifted into the cooling air. A few men smoked behind the barrels. One of them, younger, with patchy sideburns and nervous eyes, straightened when Charlie approached.

"You Randall?" he asked.

Charlie stopped. "Who's asking."

"Someone told me to pass a message," the man said, lowering his voice. "Not from Billy."

The words slid into place like a blade. "Go on," Charlie said.

The man glanced toward the kitchen windows. "Word is someone in this town keeps a book. Folks say your name's in it. Ledger, maybe. And if that ledger turns up, every man tied to it ends up in the ground before winter."

Charlie kept his face still. "Whose ledger."

The man shook his head quickly. "Didn't say. Men on the spur think you already have it. Or know where it's kept." He took a step back. "I'd leave Austin if I were you."

"Who told you my name," Charlie asked.

"I didn't ask." The man retreated another pace. "Randall… you're in something. You may not know it. But others do. And they want whatever you're carrying."

He vanished down the alley before Charlie could stop him.

The warning unsettled him more than Billy's. Billy's threat had been plain and personal, a line drawn where everyone could see it. This was different. This was whisper-work. This was a thing being shaped quietly, without faces attached.

Charlie stepped into the restaurant, threading past tables, ignoring the smell of stew and boiled onions. Heat from the kitchen washed over him as he moved down the narrow corridor. He reached the final door and paused, his hand resting against the wood.

He could hear the room before he saw it. Voices sharper tonight. Too sharp.

He pushed through.

The crowd was thinner, but the air was tighter. Runners moved with purpose. Billy watched the room with narrowed eyes, as though he expected violence. Near the back, several men Charlie did not recognize stood close together, speaking in low tones that had nothing to do with cards.

Charlie stepped inside and felt the shift immediately. Three men looked his way. One touched the brim of his hat. Another turned his back. A third simply watched, unblinking.

Billy rose halfway from his chair.

Charlie understood then. If he stayed, Billy would confront him openly. Rumor would harden into accusation. Whatever followed would not stay contained to cards and words.

So he made the only move left to him.

He did not sit. He did not linger.

He turned and walked back out, calm as a man crossing a quiet street.

No one stopped him. But he felt eyes on him all the way to the restaurant door.

Outside, the air had gone cold.

Austin had made up its mind. Someone had marked him. Someone had decided he held a ledger he had never seen. And someone wanted to be certain that whatever truth that book contained stayed buried.

Charlie tightened his coat and looked toward the dark line of hills leading south.

He had stayed in Austin as long as he dared.

The web around him was no longer tightening.

It was closing.

19

Leaving Austin

October 17 (morning), 1898 - Austin

Charlie rose before sunrise, long before the tannery whistles split the morning. Austin lay hushed under a low ceiling of fog, the kind that made a town seem to lean closer, listening. He packed quietly, rolling his shirts tight and slipping his cards into the inner pocket of his coat.

He checked the window twice for movement on the road.

None.

But absence meant nothing in Austin.

The warnings from the night before still hung in the room, heavy and unmoving. Billy's suspicion. The runner's message. Men whispering his name as if it had been loaned out without his consent. The weight of crimes that did not belong to him settling into his pockets as if they did.

He had stayed too long.

Mrs. Albright was already awake when he creaked down the stairs. She poured hot water into a coffee tin and slid it across the table without ceremony.

"You're leaving," she said. It was not a question.

"I am."

"You walking or catching a ride."

"Walking," Charlie said. "Road's clear enough."

She studied him for a moment, her gaze steady, practiced. Not fear. Not curiosity. The measured look of someone who had seen too many men pass through town carrying trouble they never spoke aloud.

“I don’t know what you stepped into,” she said, “but I do know Austin favors its own. Outsiders only win here until they don’t.”

Charlie nodded. “I appreciate the room.”

“You’d best appreciate getting out in one piece.” There was no warmth in her voice, but no malice either. Just the blunt truth of a woman shaped by this valley.

Charlie stepped into the cold morning. Fog rolled across the road in thick currents, swallowing sound. Tannery smoke bled into it, leaving a bitter tang on his tongue. The mills were only beginning to stir. A few men stood near the cookhouse drinking thin coffee. One turned as Charlie passed.

“Headed south,” Charlie said, offering nothing else.

The man grunted. “Best road for it.”

No farewell. No question. No reason to linger.

At the edge of town, Charlie slowed. He could still feel the attention he had sensed the night before. Men watching from porches. Shapes lingering in alleys. Runners who had memorized his face and carried his name to men he had never met.

Crane.
Ledger.
Debt.

None of it was his. All of it clung to him.

He reached the fork beyond the last houses. One road followed the rail line west. The other turned south toward Costello, threading between dark pines, past cold creeks and quiet farms.

Charlie paused and looked back.

Two men stood near the tannery fence. They did not wave or speak. They did not pretend to be busy. They simply watched.

That was enough.

Charlie turned south and walked.

The forest closed around him quickly. Fog thinned by degrees. Birds began to call from the trees. The ground softened underfoot as the road dipped closer to Freeman's Run. Hours passed in steady silence, broken only by the rhythm of his boots and the distant mill whistles fading behind him.

By midday he stopped at the creek. The water was cold enough to numb his fingers. He splashed his face, drank, and stood again.

He was a couple miles from Austin now. Far enough that the tightness in his shoulders began to ease.

But the name Crane did not fade. Neither did the whisper of a ledger. His steps felt aligned with something already in motion, a story begun before he knew he was part of it.

Late in the afternoon he reached the narrow bridge marking the outskirts of Costello. Smoke drifted from a handful of chimneys. Two dogs barked as he crossed. The air smelled of river mud and sawdust.

A quiet town. A place that looked, at first glance, untouched by Austin or Galeton or men who died under stories too neat to be true.

Charlie knew better than to trust first glances.

He adjusted his coat and crossed the bridge. He entered Costello with the hope that the town might grant him a few days where his name belonged to him again.

Ahead, the road curved toward the general store. The fading light seemed to fall like a line drawn across the earth.

Charlie stepped through it, leaving Austin behind.

Part 3

Costello

20

Into Costello

October 17 (late afternoon), 1898 - Costello

Costello announced itself long before Charlie reached the bridge. The air carried it. A thick, biting odor of tannins and soaked hides drifted through the trees like a warning that never quite left the valley. By the time he crossed Freeman Run and stepped onto the muddy main road, the smell had worked its way into his coat and settled there.

Costello worked because the tannery worked. Everything else bent itself around that truth.

Buildings leaned close together as if bracing against the river wind. Piles of hemlock bark rose taller than houses, stacked and restacked until they seemed permanent. Smoke lifted from the long, low stacks behind the tannery yard, where hundreds of hides soaked in pits lined with hemlock brew that stained both the ground and the men who worked it.

Charlie kept his hat low and his pace unremarkable. After Austin, the quiet here felt strange. Not welcoming, but not hostile either. Simply uninterested. Costello did not concern itself with passing strangers. It concerned itself with hides, vats, and the steady work required to keep the whole enterprise from slipping backward into the river.

A group of workers trudged past him, boots heavy with mud, aprons streaked dark with tannery residue. Their faces were pale from long hours near the pits. At the yard gate, a foreman barked orders, his voice sharp enough to cut through the low, constant hum of labor.

No one looked twice at Charlie, and that suited him.

He rented a narrow room above the general store. Mrs. Trask was thin, brisk, and sharp-eyed enough to take stock of a man by the way he set his boots down. She counted each coin twice before entering the payment into her ledger.

"You will find Costello steady," she said, closing the book. "Steady is different from safe. Keep that in mind."

Charlie nodded and said nothing. Promises, he had learned, traveled farther than a man ever intended.

For several days he walked the town without speaking unless spoken to. He traced the routes between the tannery yard and the riverbank. He learned the timing of the whistles and how far the smell drifted when the vats were stirred. He watched bark peelers move at dusk and children hop across loose planks laid over mud that never quite dried.

Most days he kept his collar high. The tannery's breath clung to everything, crept into cloth and skin alike.

By the end of the first week, he noticed the pig's ear, though not by design. It revealed itself the way such places always did. A leaning bark shed near the river, its planks warped and winter-worn, saw too much foot traffic for a structure meant to be empty. Lantern light flickered behind the boards. Men slipped in and out at irregular hours, shoulders hunched, laughter kept low and brief.

Charlie noted it and moved on. It wasn't time yet to visit the pig's ear.

He settled into a routine that asked little of him. He helped Mrs. Trask lift crates when she needed an extra hand. He returned nods from tannery men on the road and did not linger long enough to invite conversation. By the second week, even the dog stretched out on the post office porch stopped barking when he passed, accepting him as part of the scenery rather than a threat.

Peace was not something Charlie trusted. Still, Costello offered enough of its shadow that he allowed himself to breathe more easily. No rumors followed him here. No whispered use of his name. No talk of scrip or ledgers or men who vanished under the wrong kind of attention. Only the tannery's constant exhale and the rhythm of a town that endured what it had to endure.

On the final evening of his second week, frost silvered the edges of the bark piles. The river sounded sharper, thinner, as if warning winter was not far behind. Charlie found himself standing again near the leaning shed. From within came the low murmur of voices, the scrape of chairs, the soft shuffle of cards finding their way into practiced hands.

His fingers brushed the pocket where he kept his deck.

Waiting, he knew, could be a kind of hiding. And hiding never lasted.

Charlie stepped toward the crooked lantern, pushed open the warped door, and entered Costello's pig's ear for the first time.

21

The Bark-Shed Pig's Ear

October 31 (night), 1898 - Costello

The heat hit Charlie first. Not the comforting kind, but the trapped warmth of too many bodies packed into a space never meant to hold them. The bark shed's walls were thin, and the cold off Freeman Run pressed through the planks, but lanterns hung from nails in a crooked line, each throwing off more heat than light.

A dozen men crowded the interior, standing or seated wherever space allowed. Coats hung from rafters. Gloves dripped meltwater into buckets along the far wall. The air carried the permanent smell of damp wood and tannery chemicals ground into clothing by long days near the vats. Every breath tasted faintly of smoke and bark dust.

A makeshift counter ran across the back. Behind it, a stooped man poured from unlabeled bottles into tin cups. He barely glanced at Charlie. No questions. No welcome. Just another body come in from the cold. That was how a pig's ear survived in a town like Costello.

Charlie paid, nodded once, and took a small sip. The liquor burned sharp and unfinished, telling him more about its source than its quality. It loosened shoulders and warmed hands. That was all it was meant to do.

He scanned the room without turning his head.

Four card tables.
One plank laid across two barrels serving as a bar.
One stove that crackled more often than it warmed.

One doorway.
No windows.

A tight box, if trouble came.

He drifted toward the nearer table. The players did not look up. That was the unspoken rule. A stranger could exist as long as he behaved like furniture. The dealer, a broad man with a flattened nose and pale brows, slid the cards in a slow, practiced rhythm. His hands were steady. His left eye twitched when he shuffled.

Charlie watched one hand. Then another.

He listened more than he looked.

The talk stayed low, muffled by scarves and drink. Complaints about day work. Wages stretched thin. An argument between tannery foremen. A broken vat that had slowed the yard to half pace. Nothing about stolen scrip. No names he knew. No rumor sharp enough to catch on.

After Austin, the absence of danger felt almost louder than its presence.

When a seat opened, Charlie took it. No one objected. Coins clinked onto the table in small, careful stacks. No one here played large. Wages went to food and rent first. Risk came last, if at all.

Charlie matched the stakes and let the game breathe. The cards were worn soft at the corners. The table rocked when men leaned forward. The stove popped and sighed behind him.

Hours passed without friction. He won a little. Lost a little. Folded more than he played. Each choice was deliberate. He was not here to be remembered. He was here to understand.

A man survived a pig's ear by reading the room before reading the cards.

Near midnight, a draft crept through the boards, and the lantern closest to the door flickered. Men began to stand, shrugging into coats. The tannery started before daylight, and no one wanted liquor on their breath in the morning line.

Charlie finished his cup and took a final, modest pot. He pushed his chair back.

The dealer gave him a brief nod. Not friendly. Not wary. Simply acknowledgment that the stranger had played straight.

Outside, the cold felt sharper. Frost traced the edge of the shed roof. Freeman Run murmured along the bank, its voice deeper in the dark.

Charlie stood a moment, breathing the night air, letting the quiet settle where the noise had been.

Costello was not Austin. It was not Galeton either. But a pig's ear was still a pig's ear. Every one of them held a thread, if a man stayed long enough to listen.

He pulled his coat tight and walked back toward the general store. Behind him, the bark shed dimmed as the last lantern was snuffed.

Tomorrow he would return. Not to win.

To watch. To listen.

And to learn whether Costello carried even the faintest trace of the trouble that had followed his name across the valley.

22

William Hart

November 1, 1898 - Costello

Mist settled over Costello early, clinging low to the ground and blurring lantern light into soft halos. Charlie made his way toward the bark shed at an even pace, boots muffled by damp earth. The tannery had finished its day's labor, leaving the air heavy with the sour-sweet reek of hides soaking in their pits. Smoke drifted lazily from the yard, flattening itself across town like a blanket no one wanted but everyone endured.

Inside the pig's ear, the warmth closed around him at once, followed by the low hum of men easing themselves out of long hours. The room looked much as it had the night before, though more bodies pressed near the stove and the line of tin cups at the counter had doubled. Fridays did that. Pay in hand made men linger.

Charlie took a seat at the second table, keeping his profile turned and his posture loose. He played small hands, folding as often as he called, letting others take the risks. His winnings stayed light. His presence lighter still.

It was near the end of the second hour when the mood shifted.

A logger named Finch, broad-shouldered and thick with drink, slapped his cards onto the table and pointed a shaking finger at Charlie.

"You play too neat," Finch said. "Too damn neat. A man doesn't come out ahead like that without pulling something."

Charlie did not move. Accusations like that came from wounded pride more often than truth.

"I lost the hand," Charlie said quietly.

Finch slammed the table again. "You folded early. Clean. Means you knew what was coming. Means you're working angles."

Chairs scraped. A few men turned away, unwilling to be drawn in. Others leaned closer, interest sharpening. Tannery work bred strong arms and short patience. Charlie kept his hands on the table where they could be seen, palms open.

"No one is cheating," he said.

Finch pushed himself upright, swaying. "You calling me a liar."

Before Charlie could answer, another voice cut in.

"Sit down, Finch. You're past sense and headed for trouble."

A tall man stepped away from the wall near the stove and crossed the room. He moved with the steadiness of someone used to hauling weight and knowing how to place it. His canvas coat hung open, sleeves rolled back to reveal forearms lined with scars from bark knives and mill work. Dark hair, already touched with gray, framed a face that showed no fear of stepping into another man's anger.

Finch sneered. "Hart, this ain't your concern."

William Hart set a hand on Finch's shoulder. Not hard. Not gentle either. Just enough to make the choice clear.

"It becomes my concern when fists start flying in a room with one door," he said. "Sit. Or step outside. You decide."

For a moment Finch stiffened, pride fighting what little judgment he had left. Then Hart tightened his grip, barely. Finch looked around, found no one willing to back him, and dropped back into his chair with a muttered curse.

Hart held his gaze another second, then stepped away.

The room exhaled.

Charlie watched, attentive. Hart returned the look, brief but deliberate, as if measuring more than posture.

"You're new," Hart said.

"Passing through," Charlie replied.

Hart nodded. "Then pass through without taking bruises meant for other men's bad hands. Finch is tolerable sober. Liquor strips that away."

Conversation resumed, voices finding their places again. Hart took an empty chair at the edge of Charlie's table. He did not buy in. He watched the next hand play out.

After a moment, he spoke again, low.

"You handled that right. Most men bare teeth when challenged."

"No need," Charlie said.

"That's the right answer."

Hart leaned back. There was a settled weariness about him, the kind earned by too many seasons of labor and too many fights stopped before they began.

"You staying long?" Hart asked.

"A while," Charlie said. "Long enough to get my bearings."

Hart considered that. "Costello keeps quiet if you respect it. But it has edges like any place that lives off men's backs. Mind who you sit near."

Charlie nodded. "You one of the men worth minding."

A faint smile touched Hart's mouth. "Some days."

A draft slid under the door, and Hart's eyes flicked toward it.

"You came down from Austin," he said. "I can hear it in how you listen before you speak. Austin teaches that."

Charlie did not deny it.

"Men come through here carrying stories they don't share," Hart went on. "Yours looks like one of them. I'm not asking."

That earned Hart Charlie's full attention.

Hart stood and pulled on his coat. “If trouble follows you, Costello gives one warning. After that, it stops being patient.”

“And you?” Charlie asked.

Hart shrugged. “I’ve learned how to stay a step ahead of trouble. Not outrun it. Just avoid standing where it lands.”

He turned toward the door, then paused.

“One thing more. Whatever pushed you down the valley, be careful of the next town. Blowville listens harder than it should. Men there have interests deeper than cards and drink.”

Charlie felt the weight of that settle. “Speaking from experience?”

Hart hesitated, then nodded once. “I passed through Blowville. I was glad to leave.”

He opened the door, letting cold air spill into the room.

“Good luck, Randall.”

Charlie had not given his name. Yet Hart said it without edge or accusation. Only acknowledgment.

Which meant the name had already reached Costello.

Hart stepped into the mist, leaving Charlie with the noise of the pig’s ear, the echo of an unasked question, and the uneasy truth that the valley’s rumors moved faster than any man on foot.

23

Maddy Pike

November 2, 1898 - Costello

Charlie stayed away from the bark shed for two days. Cold had settled deep into the valley, laying a thin gray frost over Costello each morning. The town moved slower under it. Workers walked hunched, breath white in the air. Tannery smoke clung low, heavy enough to feel permanent, as if winter had already claimed the place.

Charlie kept to his room above the store, resting and listening to the building creak as it adjusted to the season. He slept longer than he had in weeks. On the second day he walked the length of town once, more to stretch his legs than to see anything new. By the third evening, the familiar pull returned. Not the gamble, but the rhythm. The chance to sit still and observe. The comfort of something he understood.

The bark shed glowed faintly against the frost. Ice traced the edges of its warped boards. Inside, warmth gathered in uneven pockets, the air thick with bark dust, smoke, and the sour edge of liquor poured from unmarked bottles.

Charlie took his usual place at the second table. The game moved slow at first. Then Maddy Pike appeared with her tray.

She walked with steady steps, threading between chairs without spilling a drop. Lantern light caught in her dark braid. Her eyes found his before she reached the table.

“So you came back,” she said, setting a cup in front of him.

"Rest only lasts so long," Charlie replied.

A small smile tugged at one corner of her mouth. "Some men chase rest. You look like someone who chases distraction."

"Maybe both."

"Maybe neither." Her gaze lingered, measuring him, then she moved on.

She did not go far. Each time she passed, she paused a little longer at the table, letting her hand rest a moment as she set down a cup or gathered coins. The attention was quiet, woven into glances instead of words.

At one point she leaned close enough that Charlie caught the faint scent of lavender beneath the tannery air.

"You fold too quickly," she said.

"Better to fold than to tempt Finch again."

She laughed softly. "Finch shouts his anger. He is easy. The ones to watch are the quiet men."

Her eyes held his a beat longer than necessary.

"Good thing I stay quiet," Charlie said.

"Good thing," she replied, and moved away without hiding her smile.

The game stretched toward late evening. Charlie won a little, lost a little, exactly as he meant to. When he stepped back from the table, Maddy was sweeping bark chips toward a bucket.

"Leaving already?" she asked.

"It's late."

"It's always late in here." She glanced toward the door. "There's a diner behind the post office. I go there in the mornings when I can. If you ever want something warmer than Mrs. Trask's bread, you might find me there around nine."

The invitation sat between them, plain and deliberate.

Charlie nodded once. "Maybe I will."

"You should." She turned away, but not before he saw the faint color rise in her cheeks.

Outside, frost glittered under a thin moon. Charlie walked back toward the general store with something lighter in his chest than he had felt in weeks.

He slept easily that night.

* * *

The diner was squat and narrow, its windows fogged and a stove crackling near the back wall. Charlie arrived a little past nine. Maddy already sat in a corner booth, two cups of coffee waiting as if she had never doubted him.

"You showed," she said.

"You promised better bread."

Maddy smiled.

"And besides," Charlie said as he removed his hat, "Mrs. Trask keeps count of who sleeps late."

They ordered eggs and potatoes. The food was simple but hot. Charlie found himself settling in, surprised by how easily the room quieted around her. Maddy spoke without rushing, watching the door and the other tables, noting small details as if she stored them away.

"You remind me of someone," she said at last.

"Who."

"A man named Crane. He passed through last winter. Quiet like you, but not the same kind of quiet."

Charlie's fork paused. "You knew him."

"Not well. I pour drinks. I see faces. But Crane stayed longer than most. Watched every door like a man waiting for weather to break."

"You didn't trust him."

"No." She shook her head. "Something restless in him. Like he was running from something without knowing what it was. Men like that carry trouble even when they don't mean to."

Charlie took a slow breath. "What kind of trouble."

"People started asking his name. People from other towns. The same way they've started asking about you."

The room felt smaller, though nothing had changed.

Maddy stirred her coffee. "He left sudden. No goodbyes. Some said he went north. Others said men ran him off. All I knew was the room breathed easier when he was gone."

She looked up then, steady and direct. "You're not him. But trouble circles you the same way."

"Are you warning me," Charlie asked.

"I'm asking you to be careful," she said. "For yourself. And for Costello."

Something warm settled between them, not just from the coffee or the stove. A sense of being seen without being judged.

"You're an interesting man, Randall," she said.

"I could say the same."

She laughed, lighter this time. "Then maybe we should try not to disappoint each other."

They finished slowly, talking of river ice and winter coming on. When they stepped outside, the cold bit sharp.

Maddy pulled her shawl close. "Come back to the shed tonight. I want to see how you play when you're not trying to disappear."

Charlie smiled. "Maybe I will."

"I'll see you tonight then," she said, and turned toward town.

Charlie watched her go. Then he turned toward the river, thinking not of cards or ledgers or names passed too easily between towns, but of a woman who had noticed him before he realized how much that mattered.

Costello no longer felt like a place to hide.

It felt like a place he might stay, at least a little while longer.

24

The Traveling Reverend

November 4 (night), 1898 - Costello

The bark shed breathed with a different rhythm that night. The cold had deepened, and the stove fought harder, pushing uneven waves of heat through the cramped space. Lanterns flickered along the walls, softening shadows without ever taming them. Men spoke less than usual, their voices worn down by long hours in the tannery yard.

Charlie took his usual place near the second table. He noticed Maddy before she noticed him, her braid catching the lantern light as she bent to refill a cup. She glanced his way and offered a small smile, one that eased the tightness in his chest without entirely quieting the room.

He was about to turn back to the cards when the sound at the doorway changed.

A man stepped inside who did not belong to Costello's pattern. Older, perhaps in his late fifties. Tall and spare, wrapped in a plain dark coat with the collar turned up against the cold. He was not a tannery worker. Not a woodsman. Not a drifter either.

He moved with an unhurried certainty, as if he had entered a hundred rooms just like this one and never once felt out of place.

Someone near the stove muttered, "Preacher's back."

So that was him.

The Traveling Reverend.

He carried no Bible. No visible mark of faith. No performance of piety. Just a quiet gravity that caused men to lower their cups as he passed. He nodded to no one, yet seemed to acknowledge everyone.

He stopped at Charlie's table.

"Is this seat taken," he asked.

Charlie glanced at the empty chair. "No."

The Reverend sat, folding his long hands neatly on the table. His eyes were pale and sharp, observant in a way that unsettled rather than reassured. When he spoke, his voice carried the measured calm of someone accustomed to tents, back rooms, and men who listened because they had no better choice.

"I've seen you here these past nights," he said. "You play clean."

Charlie studied him. "Do I know you."

"Not yet." The Reverend's mouth curved slightly, though the smile held no warmth. "But I make a habit of knowing men who pass through this valley. Roads teach more than sermons ever did."

The dealer pushed out a fresh hand. Charlie picked up his cards. The Reverend did not touch his.

"You don't play," Charlie said.

"I play only what's worth playing," the Reverend replied. "Tonight, cards aren't it."

"That so."

The Reverend leaned back just enough for the lantern light to catch the deep lines etched into his face. A man who had seen ruin wear many disguises and learned to recognize them all.

"Tell me something," he said. "If a ledger carried your name on its spine, but the ink belonged to another man, would you try to erase the name or find the hand that wrote it."

Charlie felt his pulse tighten, but his expression did not change. "Why ask me that."

"Because men speak," the Reverend said. "In towns north of here.

They say a name's been borrowed. They say money's moved where it should not have. And they say the sort of trouble that grows from that kind of paper does not stop with lost wages."

He paused, letting the words settle.

"A borrowed name," he went on, "can cost a man his freedom. Or his livelihood. Or his life. Depends on who comes looking first."

Charlie glanced around the room. No one appeared to be listening. Yet the Reverend spoke as though they were alone.

"Who told you this," Charlie asked.

"No one." The Reverend laid his hands flat on the table. "I listen. And when enough whispers move the same direction, I trust the wind."

He glanced at his cards for the first time, though Charlie suspected he already knew the shape of the table, the players, and the room itself.

"You're not from Costello," the Reverend continued. "Nor Austin. Nor Galeton, though your path's brushed all three."

"What path is that," Charlie asked.

"A man wearing another man's name," the Reverend said calmly. "A ledger that balances more than accounts. A circle of men who fear daylight more than the law. And someone standing where they can be seen when the blame needs a face."

The Reverend slid his untouched cards back to the dealer.

"I'm not here to accuse you," he said. "Only to remind you that valleys remember names long after towns forget faces."

Maddy appeared at Charlie's shoulder with a fresh cup. She hesitated when she saw who sat with him.

"Evening, Reverend," she said carefully.

"Miss Pike," he replied, inclining his head.

"You need anything," she asked.

"Only clarity," he said.

She frowned slightly and moved on, casting a questioning look at Charlie before returning to the counter.

The Reverend stood.

"I travel south tomorrow," he said. "Toward Blowville. If you're wise, you'll travel slower than I do. Some ground needs time before it's safe to cross."

"What waits there," Charlie asked.

The Reverend shook his head. "A man named Crane walked this valley once with ambition in his pockets and fear at his heels. He left marks behind him. Marks men thought time would wash away."

He turned toward the door.

"If you follow that trail," he said, "keep your eyes open. Paper cuts deeper than steel when the right hands are holding it."

Then he stepped out into the cold.

Charlie remained seated long after the door closed, the cards lying untouched before him, the heat of the bark shed pressing against a truth that felt colder than the night outside.

Crane.
Blowville.
A ledger that promised ruin depending on who believed what was written inside it.

And a man who treated whispers like scripture.

25

Quiet Days, Quiet Games

November 5, 1898 - Costello

The next several days settled into a pattern that felt almost peaceful. Almost.

Costello in early November moved slowly toward winter. Frost clung to the grass each dawn. The tannery smoke rose thick and steady, flattening itself across the roofs and pressing the valley low. Workers walked with collars turned up and heads bowed, carrying the cold with them from yard to yard.

Charlie let the town slow him.

He had learned long ago that questions often cost more than they returned. A man who asked too much made himself part of the story, and stories in towns like this had a way of settling on whoever stood closest. Better to listen. Better to watch how money moved, who stayed too long at a table, who left too soon, who drank enough to loosen his tongue and who drank only enough to keep warm.

When a place began to make sense, that was usually when it was time to go.

He slept longer than he had in weeks. He walked more. He listened to Costello breathe, learning its pauses and habits, the hours when the tannery road filled, the lull after supper, the slow drift toward the bark shed once the day's work was done.

Most mornings found him at the small diner behind the post office, and most mornings Maddy Pike was already there. She sat at the same corner table with a cup held between her hands, steam lifting toward the window and fogging the glass. When she saw him step inside, she lifted her chin in greeting, her smile quiet but certain.

“Morning,” she would say.

“Morning,” he would answer.

Some days they spoke about the weather or the tannery yard. Some days they spoke about nothing at all. The silence between them was easy, the kind that did not need filling and did not ask to be explained.

One morning Maddy pushed her half-finished coffee aside.

“You walk the river much,” she asked.

“Sometimes.”

“Walk it with me,” she said. “I do not care for sitting still all day.”

So they followed the narrow path along Freeman Run. Brown leaves gathered in the eddies. The cold water carried a steady murmur, almost like speech if a man listened long enough. Maddy walked with sure steps, pulling her shawl closer, her braid brushing the front of her coat. She never pressed Charlie for answers, and he did not offer more than he intended. That seemed to suit her.

“You are quieter than most men who pass through,” she said once.

“Does that bother you.”

“It might,” she said. “If you were dull. But you are not dull.”

She said it as if it were a settled fact. Charlie had no answer ready, and she did not wait for one. She only kept walking, boots brushing frost from the grass at the edge of the path.

By the time they reached the bend in the river, her hands were pink from the cold. Charlie offered his gloves. She refused at first, then accepted them a moment later, laughing softly at her own stubbornness.

“They will be too big,” she said.

“They will still help,” he replied.

She looked at him with a softness he had not expected, then slipped her fingers into the gloves and walked on without another word.

* * *

Each evening he returned to the bark shed.

Not because he was short on coin, nor because he needed the game. The place had simply worked itself quietly into his days.

The games were modest. Tannery wages did not stretch far. Charlie played the second table most nights, folding when sense told him to, pressing only when the odds gave him permission. Men here did not gamble for ruin. They gambled to dull the ache left by long hours breathing tannins and standing over vats that soaked into a man's clothes and seemed never quite to leave him.

Maddy moved through the room with her usual ease, her tray balanced as if it were part of her. She slipped between shoulders without brushing a coat. Each time she passed Charlie's table, her hand lingered near his cup, never quite touching him, but near enough that he noticed.

"How quiet you are tonight," she said once.

"Quiet rooms make quiet men," Charlie answered.

Her smile curved slightly. "Quiet rooms also hide storms."

He felt her meaning more than he understood it. Or perhaps he understood it and did not want to test it. She walked away before he could ask.

Later that night, as she gathered empty cups, Charlie joined her near the stove. Heat brushed against both of them and softened the chill that seemed to live in the boards.

"You walk the river again tomorrow," she asked.

"If you like."

"I do."

The answer was simple, but something in the way she said it stayed with him after she moved away.

* * *

Their walks became part of the rhythm too. Short loops along the mill road. Crossings near the old footbridge. Coffee afterward, hands wrapped around warm cups while the town stirred itself awake around them.

One morning they sat on the low wall beside the diner as men passed on their way to work. Maddy shivered and leaned a little closer to him, not enough to make a statement. Just enough to borrow warmth.

“You do not smile much,” she said.

“Never found much reason.”

“Maybe you should start,” she said. “Men who forget joy forget half their steps.”

He looked at her. “You sound like someone who has practiced that line.”

“I have,” she admitted with a grin. “But it is still true.”

For a brief moment, he smiled. It came easier than he expected. That frightened him more than the cold ever had.

She saw it and made no effort to hide that it pleased her.

That, more than the words, stayed with him.

* * *

But the quiet carried an edge.

The Traveling Reverend did not return. Men spoke of him anyway, voices lowered, repeating his words as if they feared them. Rumors of borrowed names and hidden accounts brushed through town like cold drafts under a door. No one said much plainly. They only circled the ideas, touched them, then moved off as though afraid of being seen standing too near.

Charlie walked more during the day, pacing Costello’s narrow streets as if searching for something he could not name. He watched freight wagons rattle toward the tannery. He listened for familiar voices and heard none. Still, the Reverend’s warning clung to him, a thought he could not shake.

Mrs. Trask noticed.

"You are restless," she said while stacking cans behind the counter.

"Am I."

"You have the look of a man waiting on news he does not wish to hear."

He did not answer. She did not expect one. She only reached for another can and set it into place with more force than the task required.

* * *

One evening at the pig's ear, Maddy set a cup down in front of him and leaned closer than usual.

"You are thinking too hard again," she said.

"Maybe."

"You will wear grooves into your thoughts if you keep pacing them. Let the cards do the work for a while."

Her eyes were warm in the lantern light. Her smile eased the tightness between his shoulders in a way the whiskey never could.

"You are better company than the cards," he said quietly.

Maddy's breath caught, just a little. "Good," she said. "I hoped that was true."

She moved away with a lightness in her step, though she glanced back at him more than once. Charlie watched her go, then looked down at his hand and realized he had not truly seen the cards in front of him.

* * *

No trouble came that night. Nor the next. Nor the one after.

Yet the valley felt changed. As if something had begun shifting beneath the frost, too deep to see plainly, but near enough to feel.

Charlie felt it. Maddy sensed it too. Even William Hart watched the door more often than before, his gaze lifting whenever the latch moved or a draft slipped in under the boards.

Quiet days. Quiet games. And beneath them, a pressure slowly building.

Charlie kept playing cards. He kept walking the river with Maddy and sharing coffee in the mornings, studying her smile as the frost crept higher each day and the valley drew itself tighter around its own silences.

But he understood the truth.

Peace was never meant to last. Not for him.

Not in this valley.

And before long, the quiet would break.

26

Cullen Pratt Arrives

November 15, 1898 - Costello

The cold had hardened into something sharp by mid November. Frost clung to every rail, every shed roof, every low branch along Freeman Run. Smoke from the tannery stacks drifted in slow, heavy ribbons that barely moved in the still air. Charlie felt the shift the moment he stepped outside that morning. The valley was waiting for something. He did not know what.

The diner was quieter than usual. Maddy sat alone in their corner booth with a cup held between her hands. She smiled when he joined her, but the smile did not quite reach her eyes.

"You sense it," she said softly.

"Town feels different," Charlie replied.

"Tight," she said. "Like someone pulled a cord around it in the night." She glanced toward the window. "Even the tannery boys came in without a word. That has not happened once since you arrived."

He listened. She was right. Men moved with careful restraint, the way loggers approached thin ice. Cups touched tables gently. A pair of bark peelers kept glancing toward the door as if expecting it to open.

Maddy lowered her voice. "I do not like it."

"Maybe just the season," Charlie said.

"No," she answered. "This is something else."

After breakfast they walked the river path, though the wind cut harder along the banks. Maddy tucked her hands beneath her shawl. Charlie offered his gloves and she accepted them with a small, grateful smile. Freeman Run moved under a thin skin of ice along the edges, whispering against the stones.

"Whatever is coming," she said, "I hope it passes by us."

Charlie wished he believed that. Trouble had a habit of traveling the same roads he did. He had learned to read the signs.

* * *

Evening came early. The bark shed glowed with lantern light long before supper. Men entered more slowly than usual, eyes lingering on the shadows outside before stepping in. Rumors moved through the room in fragments. A rider seen near the tannery road. A stranger at the blacksmith shop asking questions that did not belong to him.

Charlie took his place at the second table. William Hart stood near the stove, posture stiff, watching the door. Maddy moved between tables, but each time the latch lifted she paused, breath caught for a beat too long.

It happened near the end of the first hour.

The door opened and a rush of cold swept into the shed, snuffing the lantern nearest the entrance.

A man stepped inside.

Tall. Broad across the shoulders. A coat cleaner than any tannery worker would keep. Boots free of bark mud and yard grime.

The stranger's eyes moved with deliberate precision, as if he had followed a trail for days and had finally reached its end.

Cullen Pratt.

The room fell quiet, not by choice but by instinct.

Cullen's gaze passed over the tables, unhurried and certain. When it reached Charlie, it held. Long enough for the air to thin.

He went to the counter, spoke quietly to the barkeeper, then glanced toward Charlie when the man gestured in his direction.

Maddy froze mid-step, tension rising in her shoulders.

Cullen crossed the room and stopped beside Charlie's table.

"Evening," he said. His voice was smooth, controlled, and carried a weight that made the card players straighten.

Charlie looked up. "Evening."

"Name."

"Randall."

A small smile touched Cullen's mouth. Almost satisfied. "Good. Saves time."

He sat without asking. He brought no cards, no coin, no pretense of play. William Hart shifted near the stove, alert but still.

Cullen studied Charlie with an even, appraising gaze.

"I have been looking for you," he said. "You have left quite a trail."

"I do not know you," Charlie replied.

"You will," Cullen said. "There is a matter requiring your attention. A ledger. A man who wrote your name beside sums that were never earned."

Charlie kept his hands flat on the table. His pulse remained steady, though his thoughts sharpened. "That sounds like someone else's lie."

"It is," Cullen agreed. "But the lie points your way. And I am here to see where that road leads."

He rose with measured control.

"Put your affairs in order," he said. "I will come again. When I do, we will finish the business already begun."

He left without waiting for an answer.

For several heartbeats no one spoke. The lantern by the door flickered back to life. Maddy stepped closer to Charlie, her voice low.

"Who was that."

"Trouble," Charlie said.

"You said you were done with trouble."

"So I did."

She touched his sleeve, her fingers cold. "Please be careful."

Charlie nodded. The valley had shifted. Costello was no longer a refuge. Cullen Pratt had seen to that.

And from the look in his eyes, this was only the beginning.

* * *

Charlie watched the door long after Cullen was gone. The cold seemed reluctant to leave with him. Cards lay untouched. No one picked up their hands.

William Hart finally stepped away from the stove.

He crossed the room with steady purpose, the kind that did not draw attention yet changed the air. Maddy retreated toward the counter, giving them space.

William stopped beside Charlie's table and rested a hand on the back of the empty chair Cullen had used, as if testing how much of the man remained.

"You want to tell me what that was," he said.

"Wish I could," Charlie replied.

William studied him. Lantern light caught the creases at the corners of his eyes. He had lived long enough to recognize trouble by its outline.

"That man was not here for a drink," William said.

"I noticed."

"He was not here for cards either. Men who come to play look at the tables first. He looked at faces. Then he walked straight to you."

Charlie stayed silent.

"I have seen men like him," William continued. "They push others into corners and wait to see how they move. But this one came with a list, and your name was already on it."

Charlie felt the truth of that settle.

William pulled out the chair and sat across from him. Around them the game dissolved quietly, chips left where they lay.

"You have been careful since you arrived," William said. "That makes people notice. When a stranger walks in and singles you out, it makes men uneasy."

"Let them wonder," Charlie said.

"Wondering is not the danger," William replied. "Fear is. And that man carries it. Like someone who lost something and intends to reclaim it."

Charlie looked toward the door. Frost had already begun to creep back across the windowpane.

"You ever heard the name Cullen Pratt," he asked.

William shook his head. "No. But I know what kind of man can still a room without raising his voice. Purpose makes men dangerous."

Charlie exhaled slowly.

William stood. "If you need a word passed or a place watched, you come find me." He paused. "Costello looks after those who do not bring trouble on purpose."

"Thank you," Charlie said.

William nodded once and returned to the stove.

The bark shed slowly regained its sound, thinner now, stretched across an unease no one named. Maddy watched Charlie from behind the counter, worry set hard in her face.

Charlie stepped outside where the cold cut clean. Freeman Run whispered beneath its thin skin of ice.

Cullen Pratt had come to Costello. And the shape of the valley had changed.

27

Cullen's Accusation

November 16, 1898 - Costello

Snow threatened all morning, drifting in thin, restless flurries that never fully took hold. The tannery whistles cut sharp through the cold, sending workers along the muddy streets with their collars pulled high. Charlie kept to the quieter paths, hoping Cullen Pratt had taken his measure and moved on.

By afternoon, he knew better.

Charlie had just settled into a cup of coffee at the diner when the door flew open. The place was nearly empty. Maddy was off for the day, and the quiet felt like another warning. A boy burst inside, breathless, eyes wide.

"You staying over Mrs. Trask's," the boy asked.

Charlie stiffened. "Who wants to know."

"He said to fetch you," the boy replied. "Said if you do not come out, he will come in."

Charlie set the cup down. "Where is he."

"By the river path. Near the tannery road." The boy swallowed. "Sir, he looked serious."

Charlie paid and stepped back into the cold. The air bit harder than the morning had promised. The sky lay low and gray, heavy enough to press the town down another inch. He walked toward Freeman Run, boots crunching through a thin crust of frost.

Cullen waited near the split cedar fence that bordered the narrow trail. One hand rested on the rail as he looked out over the water. From a distance he might have seemed calm, almost reflective. Charlie knew better. Some men wore calm the way others wore armor.

Cullen turned at the sound of footsteps.

"Randall," he said.

"What is this about," Charlie asked.

"You know what it is about."

Charlie stopped a few paces short. "You followed me from Austin."

"And Galeton before it," Cullen said. "Chasing the name you carry. Chasing what followed it."

"I do not carry anyone's trouble."

"That so."

Cullen reached into his coat. Charlie's muscles tightened, but Cullen drew out only a folded page. He opened it slowly.

Ledger ink. Dates. Amounts. And a name written with deliberate pressure.

Charles Randall.

Cullen tapped the page once with his gloved finger. "My brother had this when he died. Kept it close before that. Said the man named here would help him clear a debt. A bad one."

Charlie did not move. "I never met your brother."

Cullen studied him. "Luke Pratt. That name mean anything to you."

It did not.

"He ran messages north of Galeton," Cullen continued. "Worked for men who paid in scrip and silence. He told me once he was buried deeper than he meant to be, but that he had found a way out. Said Charles Randall would fix it."

Charlie shook his head. "Someone lied to him."

Cullen's eyes hardened. "Luke died with his skull split open. They called it a fall. Said he slipped on wet stone. Convenient."

The cold between them deepened.

"I am sorry for your loss," Charlie said. "But I had nothing to do with it."

Cullen stepped closer. The space narrowed to something dangerous.

"Someone used your name," Cullen said. "My brother trusted that name. Trusted it enough to stake his life on it. He paid for that trust."

Charlie kept his voice even. "Then whoever used my name put both of us in danger."

For the first time, Cullen smiled. There was no warmth in it. "That is the first honest thing you have said."

He folded the page and slid it back into his coat.

"Here is what I know," Cullen said. "Luke was tied to Goodyear scrip. Something illegal. Something worth killing over. Before he died, he wrote about a man named Crane. Said Crane vouched for Randall. Said if he found Randall, the rest would fall into place."

Charlie felt his breath catch, though his face remained still.

Crane. Again.

"I do not know Crane," Charlie said.

"Yet everywhere I follow that name, yours sits beside it," Cullen replied. "So either you are lying, or Crane dragged you into something you refuse to see."

Charlie said nothing.

Cullen straightened. "I will find the truth. With or without you. But if I learn you had any hand in my brother's death, I will put you in the ground beside him."

The words were quiet. They were not a threat. They were a promise.

Charlie met his gaze. "If I learn anything that clears your brother's name, you will hear it."

Cullen nodded once. "Good. Then we start even."

He stepped back. "But hear this. If you run, I will follow. If you lie, I will know. And if Crane shows himself, you had better choose carefully which side you stand on."

Cullen turned toward the road. Snow began to fall in thin, drifting flakes, softening his shape until he faded into the gray.

Charlie watched him go.

The valley had been restless all morning. Now he understood why.

Cullen Pratt had come for answers.

And he would not leave until he had them.

28

Name in the Ledger

November 17, 1898 - Costello

Snow thickened overnight, settling into the grooves of the boardwalk and along the rooflines of the tannery sheds. The town moved under a muted hush, as if even Freeman Run hesitated before finding its course. Charlie spent the morning walking the river's edge, trying to give shape to Cullen Pratt's words, but every path his thoughts took bent back to the same knot.

Crane.
The ledger.
The name that was not his, yet had fastened itself to him all the same.

By late afternoon he returned to the bark shed. A few men had already gathered near the stove, clapping their hands to chase the cold from their fingers. Maddy moved between tables with her usual quiet competence, though Charlie caught the brief flicker of relief in her eyes when she saw him. William Hart nodded once from his place near the far wall.

Charlie chose a corner table. He did not come to gamble. He came to listen.

It did not take long.

The Reverend arrived as the lamps were being trimmed. No one knew if he had ever preached a sermon, and no one asked. He played cards with the measured calm of a man accustomed to weighing consequences. Tonight he carried a small leather notebook tied with twine.

He came straight to Charlie's table.

"Mind if I sit," he asked.

Charlie motioned to the open chair.

"There is talk in town," the Reverend said as he settled in. "A stranger has been asking for you."

Charlie said nothing.

The Reverend rested his fingers on the notebook. "Talk usually starts somewhere."

"Usually," Charlie replied.

For a moment they let the room speak instead. Cards snapped against wood. Coins slid and settled. The stove cracked sharply as the cold pressed against its iron skin.

At last, the Reverend untied the twine and opened the notebook. Inside were copied ledger figures, written in a steady, disciplined hand.

"These are not originals," he said. "Those are scattered. Some burned. Some hidden. Some held by men who mistake possession for protection. I keep what I can."

Charlie remained still.

The Reverend turned a page and pushed the notebook toward him.

Written clean and dark across the line was a name.

CHARLES RANDALL.

"This is not your hand," the Reverend said.

"No."

"And not your account."

"No."

"Then we understand each other."

Charlie leaned back slightly. "Where did it come from."

"From a man who wanted into a system he only half understood," the Reverend said. “A man who believed speed could replace caution.”

The name surfaced in Charlie’s mind before it was spoken.

“Crane,” the Reverend said. “From Blowville.”

Charlie nodded once. “He used my name.”

“Repeatedly,” the Reverend replied. “A stranger with no roots makes a useful mask. A gambler’s name even more so. Men expect lies to follow gamblers. It saves effort.”

Charlie closed the notebook. “Why tell me now.”

“Because the man who borrowed your name is no longer here to answer for it.” The Reverend folded his hands. “Word is he reached too high, too quickly. Someone objected.”

“Dead.”

“Perhaps. Or hiding.” The Reverend’s voice did not change. “Men vanish in these valleys without ceremony.”

Charlie traced the notebook’s edge with his thumb. “Cullen Pratt’s brother trusted that name. Trusted the wrong man.”

The Reverend inclined his head. “It happens often. Wrong trust. Wrong name. Wrong hour.”

Charlie glanced across the shed. Maddy watched from behind the counter, concern drawn into the set of her mouth. William Hart watched as well, quieter, weighing.

The Reverend lowered his voice. “You would be wise to leave Costello soon. The men behind this scrip business are unsettled. And unsettled men keep blades close.”

“I know,” Charlie said.

“Then go quickly,” the Reverend replied. “And quietly.”

He stood, tied the notebook shut, and gathered it back into his coat.

“One more thing,” he said.

Charlie waited.

"Crane was clever, but not careful. His ambition outran his judgment. That is why his lies have become another man's danger."

With that, the Reverend stepped away and folded back into the room's uneven hum.

Charlie remained seated, letting the truth settle into place.

Crane had forged the entries.
Crane had used his name.
Crane had drawn Cullen Pratt's grief and fury down onto him like weather over open ground.

Outside, the snow fell heavier, thick flakes dissolving into the churned mud beyond the door. The valley felt smaller now, its shadows repeating shapes he had already learned to recognize.

Charlie knew then that Costello could not hold him much longer.

And wherever he went next, Crane's shadow would follow.

29

Dangerous Dispute

November 18, 1898 - Costello

Morning came gray and heavy, the kind of light that made the tannery roofs look bowed under their own weight. Charlie spent the early hours walking the length of the river path, trying to shake the unease left behind by the Reverend's visit. Crane had used his name. That truth had weight. And somewhere behind it lay the reason Cullen Pratt had followed him this far south.

By midday he returned to town, keeping to the alleys behind the shops. Costello felt altered. Men spoke less freely. Strangers were watched longer. Even Mrs. Pike lowered her voice when Charlie stopped in for tea.

"You stir trouble without meaning to," she said.

"I am learning," Charlie replied.

She nodded once and returned to her work, as if there was nothing more to say that would help either of them.

Snow began falling by evening, slow and thick, softening the edges of the streets. Charlie headed toward the bark shed, not out of comfort but out of habit. Staying still felt like an invitation now.

Inside, the room carried a restless edge. The stove clattered as it worked against the cold. Men shook snow from their coats and crowded the tables, their attention sharp in a way that had little to do with cards.

Maddy reached him as he took a seat.

"You look worn," she said.

"Long day."

"You ought to leave town soon."

"I will."

Maddy hesitated, touched his arm lightly, and moved on without a word.

The first game of the night formed at the far table. The pot grew faster than it should have, driven by pride more than coin. Charlie watched from where he sat, hands folded, eyes taking measure.

Voices rose.

Two tannery men argued over a hand, one accusing the other of palming a card. Chairs scraped. The tension flared quick and dry, like bark catching flame.

Charlie stayed quiet. He had no part in it, but the argument widened, pulling eyes with it.

The heavier of the two men jabbed a finger at his opponent. "You cheat again and I break your hand."

"No one here cheats but you," the other snapped back.

Men leaned away, giving the fight room. William Hart's gaze flicked toward Charlie, as if he sensed the shift before it arrived.

Then the heavier man turned and pointed across the shed.

"Ask him," he shouted. "Randall. He watches every hand in this place."

The room stilled.

Charlie felt the weight of the attention settle on him, heavy and unwelcome.

"I did not see the play," he said.

"That is not good enough," the man replied, stepping closer. "You sit here night after night, eyes sharp as a blade. Tell us who cheated."

"I cannot," Charlie said.

The man closed the distance another step. “Maybe you will not. Maybe you are hiding something.”

A voice near the stove muttered, “Saw him talking with the Reverend.”

Another followed. “Pratt came looking for him. That alone says enough.”

Charlie stood, slow and deliberate, palms open. “This is not my quarrel.”

The tannery worker’s face flushed. “Everything feels like your quarrel since you came here. Trouble in Galeton. Trouble in Austin. Now strangers with hard eyes asking for you. Makes a man wonder what you dragged in behind you.”

Charlie did not answer. The room had already decided how it wanted to hear him.

The man seized a lantern and lifted it, throwing light across Charlie’s face. The flame flickered, shadows breaking and reforming.

“Look at him,” he said. “Does he look like someone passing through. Or someone carrying something with him.”

Before the moment could harden further, Maddy stepped forward and set the lantern back on the table.

“That is enough,” she said. “You do not get to turn a card game into a hanging just because you are angry.”

Her hand shook, but her voice held.

William Hart pushed through the men with quiet authority. “He gave you his answer. Let it stand.”

The tannery worker hesitated, breath heavy, fists tight. For a moment it seemed he might strike anyway. Then he spat on the floor, muttered a curse, and backed away.

The fight drained out of the room, leaving behind a brittle quiet. Men returned to their tables, though no one relaxed. The bark shed found its noise again, thinner and strained.

Maddy came close to Charlie. "You need to go. Not tomorrow. Tonight."

She said it like a decision she was forcing herself to survive.

Charlie nodded. "I know."

He stepped back into the cold. Snow had begun to cover the path, smoothing the ground, softening the town's hard lines. But nothing about the night felt gentle.

Costello was no longer a refuge.

It felt like a door easing shut.

And Charlie was still on the wrong side of it.

30

Fire in the Bark Shed

November 19 (night), 1898 - Costello

Snow deepened through the night, smoothing the ruts in the road and softening Costello's sounds until the town felt drawn inward, held tight by cold. Charlie walked back to his rented room with his collar turned up, his thoughts circling the same hard truth.

He could not stay.

Costello had been a shelter for a short while, but Cullen Pratt's arrival had poisoned the ground beneath his feet. Crane's lies had traveled too far, touched too many men. Now the danger moved with him, quiet and patient.

He lit the lamp inside his narrow room. The cot, the washstand, the single chair all looked smaller than they had before, like borrowed things waiting to be reclaimed. He packed slowly. Shirts folded. Coat rolled. Coins counted and tucked deep into his satchel. When he lifted the bedroll, frost slipped from the window ledge and brushed his knuckles.

He paused.

Leaving did not feel like escape. It felt like stepping deeper into a story already written. But Blowville was the only place Crane's shadow made sense. If answers existed, they would be there.

Charlie slung the satchel over his shoulder and stepped back into the cold.

The bark shed glowed faintly at the edge of town, lantern light trembling through warped boards. He went not for cards or company, but for Maddy Pike. He did not want to leave Costello without seeing her once more.

Inside, the warmth carried a sharp edge. Fewer men had returned after the earlier dispute. A pair sat close to the stove, boots steaming. The dealer shuffled with care, the sound dry and cautious, as if the room itself might break if pushed too far.

Maddy saw Charlie the moment he entered. She crossed quickly, worry tightening her posture.

"You should not be here," she whispered. "Not after earlier."

"I am not staying," Charlie said. "I came to tell you."

She steadied the tray against her hip. "Tell me."

"You were right," he said. "About leaving. About not waiting."

Her eyes widened just slightly. "You are going tonight."

"Tonight," he said. "Before trouble finds me again. Or finds someone standing too close."

She exhaled, a breath caught between relief and fear. "Good. You should have gone the moment that man stepped into town."

"I wanted you to know," Charlie said. "Did not feel right to disappear."

She studied him, lips pressed together. "And what did you hope I would say, Charlie Randall."

He hesitated. "That you might wait for me. Or that you might think about coming with me."

A small, aching smile touched her mouth. "I cannot leave. Not like that. But I will wait. I will want to know you are still walking."

Charlie nodded. She brushed his sleeve, her hand lingering just long enough to matter.

"You head south," she said. "And you watch yourself in Blowville. That town hides its truths crooked. Crane proved that."

Before Charlie could answer, a shout cut through the shed.

"Smoke."

The cry came from the back wall. Heads turned. A thin gray ribbon curled upward between the boards.

“Check the stove,” someone called.

But the stove was clear.

“Fire,” another voice shouted. “Behind the wall.”

Men surged to their feet. The dealer swept cards from the table. Smoke thickened fast, lantern light turning hazy and dull.

Then someone yelled, “The door will not open.”

Charlie moved without thinking. He pushed through the crowd to the entrance. The latch rattled under his hand, stiff and unmoving.

Not frozen.

Barred.

“Who locked this,” Charlie shouted.

A man beside him coughed, doubled over. Another kicked at the boards. Flames climbed the far wall, feeding on old bark scraps piled too close.

“Break it,” Charlie said.

Shoulders slammed into the door. It groaned but held. Smoke rolled in heavier now, hot and bitter. Panic rippled. A table overturned. A lantern shattered, flame racing along the floor.

Charlie felt a grip on his arm. Maddy’s voice came through the smoke.

“Help me get them to the back.”

He guided her and three others toward the rear window. William Hart was already there, swinging a length of pipe against the frame. Wood split. Cold air rushed in.

“Out,” William called. “One at a time.”

Charlie lifted a coughing man through, then another. A third climbed out on his own. Fire roared along the wall nearest the stove, swallowing the corner in orange light.

“Go,” Maddy urged. “You go now.”

Charlie shook his head. “I will finish here.”

“The fire is moving fast,” she said.

Another man staggered toward them. Charlie caught him and shoved him toward the opening. Smoke clawed at his throat. Heat pressed close enough to burn.

“Maddy,” he said. “Go.”

She hesitated, then climbed through.

Only a few men remained. Charlie hauled one toward the window, then another. Sparks drifted down like burning snow.

William’s voice cut through from outside. “Last one.”

Charlie took two steps toward the opening.

The ceiling groaned.

A heavy timber shifted overhead. The window frame warped inward. William reached in, trying to wrench it free, but fire had already taken the rafters.

“Charlie, move,” William shouted.

Charlie turned toward the door instead. The flames might have weakened it. It was the only chance left.

He drove his shoulder into the boards.

Nothing.

Heat surged. Sparks stung his skin. Breathing felt like swallowing fire.

Outside, voices shouted for water. For help.

Inside, the air narrowed to pain.

Charlie stepped back, braced himself, and threw his full weight into the door.

It held.

The bark shed burned around him.

Charlie Randall was trapped.

31

Cornered by Cullen

November 19 (night), 1898 - Costello

Smoke thickened until the rafters blurred into shadow. Heat rolled through the bark shed in heavy waves, each stronger than the last. Charlie pulled his sleeve over his mouth and tried the door again. The boards held. The latch would not give. Flames licked along the frame, testing it.

He stepped back, blinking through the sting in his eyes, searching for one last path out.

Something moved inside the smoke.

Charlie froze.

The shape sharpened as firelight flared behind it, a man stepping forward with a slow, deliberate pace, untouched by panic.

Cullen Pratt stepped through the smoke with a steadiness that did not belong in a burning room.

He did not cough. He did not shield his eyes. He glanced once toward the rafters, then toward the far wall, as if taking the measure of the fire rather than fearing it.

His coat was dusted with sparks. His face was calm in a way that did not belong in a burning room.

"Seems you got yourself cornered," Cullen said.

Charlie coughed, breath tearing at his chest. "Get out. The roof is coming down."

Cullen kept walking. “Not until this is finished.”

Charlie backed toward the far wall. The floor groaned underfoot. A beam overhead split with a sharp crack.

“Pratt,” Charlie said, forcing his voice steady, “if you want answers, killing me will not give them to you.”

“I am not here for answers,” Cullen said. “I am here for truth. A man shows it when there is nowhere left to run.”

He stepped closer, eyes fixed on Charlie through the smoke.

“You run from fire the same way you run from everything else,” Cullen said. “That tells me enough.”

Charlie set his feet. “You think I killed your brother.”

“I think you know who did,” Cullen said. “And you have been carrying that knowledge quietly.”

A burning strip of bark dropped between them. Charlie turned his face away as embers scattered.

“You are hunting the wrong man,” Charlie said. “Your brother trusted someone who used my name. A man from Blowville. Crane.”

Cullen did not flinch, but something tightened at the edges of his eyes.

“Crane,” Charlie said again. “He forged the ledger. He pulled your brother into the scrip trade. He lied about me. Luke died because of him, not because of me.”

The shed groaned louder. Fire chewed along the ceiling beams. William’s voice shouted from outside, but the roar swallowed it whole.

Cullen took another step. “You speak easily for a man choking on smoke.”

Charlie reached down and seized a half burned board, gripping it as the heat bit at his skin.

“I do not want to fight you,” Charlie said.

“Then tell me where Crane is,” Cullen said.

“He vanished,” Charlie said. “Weeks ago. Before I ever knew your name. Before your brother died.”

“Men do not vanish,” Cullen said. “They get buried.”

Another beam cracked. The ceiling sagged lower.

For the first time, Cullen glanced upward.

“You keep talking,” he said, “but nothing sounds like truth.”

Charlie saw the opening.

“If you want what really happened to your brother,” Charlie said, “then follow me out of here. Follow me to Blowville. That is where Crane lived. That is where his trail leads.”

Fire roared as if answering him.

Cullen hesitated, shifting his weight, half a step toward the darker side of the shed, where the heat had not yet taken full hold.

Only a breath, but it was enough.

Charlie threw himself at the door again, shoulder first. The boards splintered. A second strike tore loose the lower hinge. Cold air rushed in hard, dragging smoke with it.

Charlie forced his way through the gap.

Behind him, the ceiling gave way. A beam crashed down between them, flames curling high around it.

Cullen leapt back as the fire surged.

Charlie stumbled into the cold night, coughing hard, eyes burning. William Hart caught his arm and hauled him clear as the doorway sagged inward.

“You alive,” William said, voice tight.

“Mostly,” Charlie rasped.

The bark shed buckled with a deep, settling roar. Flame burst through the roof as men shouted and formed a line toward the pump.

Maddy pushed through the crowd and grabbed Charlie’s sleeve, holding him as if he might slip away. "I thought you were gone," she said.

Charlie squeezed her hand once. "Not yet."

He looked back at the burning shed.

Through smoke and flame, Cullen did not emerge.

But Charlie had seen enough of the man to know the truth.

A fire like that did not kill someone who walked into it without fear.

Cullen Pratt was still alive.

And he would not stop.

32

Escape into the First Fork

November 19 (night), 1898 - Costello

Night closed in hard around Costello. The burning bark shed cast a red, wavering glow against the trees while men shouted and worked the pump, throwing bucket after bucket of water across the snow. Steam rose in thick bursts, hissing where it struck hot wood. The fire would die eventually, but the building was already lost.

Charlie stood at the edge of the crowd, chest burning, breath ragged from smoke. His satchel hung heavy at his side, damp where sparks had settled and died. He looked back once, expecting to see Cullen among the men spilling into the snow.

He did not.

But he also did not see a body carried out. No shape dragged clear of the smoke. Nothing that felt like an ending.

Maddy caught his arm again. "Go," she said. "Slip out while they are all watching the fire."

"I will come back when I can," Charlie said.

"Just go and be safe." Her hand stayed on his sleeve a beat too long, fingers tightening as if she meant to hold him there. He let it, just for that moment, as if the weight of it might carry with him.

Then he nodded once and pulled free.

Leaving the firelight, he cut across the river path, keeping to the shadows behind the tannery sheds. Snow crunched softly beneath his boots. Smoke followed him, clinging to his coat, mixing with the sharp, ever-present bite of tannin in the air. The town behind him roared and shifted, but ahead there was only dark.

At the far edge of town, he reached the narrow footbridge over First Fork. The river below ran dark and fast, its surface broken by thin blades of ice that caught the firelight and vanished again. He rested a hand on the rail, steadying himself, feeling the tremor in his fingers more than seeing it.

He drew one breath. Then another. A sound behind him stopped him cold.

Footsteps.

Slow. Even. Certain.

Charlie turned.

At the far end of the bridge, half lit by the distant glow of the fire, stood Cullen Pratt.

His coat hung open. Soot streaked his face. He looked untouched by the chaos behind him, as if the burning shed had been no more than a delay, something to step through on his way here.

"I don't think we are finished, Randall," Cullen said.

Charlie glanced over the rail. The drop was steep. Rocks waited below before the current could take him. A fall like that could break him just as easily as it could save him.

"I do not want to fight you," Charlie said.

"You keep saying that," Cullen replied, stepping onto the bridge. The boards creaked beneath his weight, each step carrying through the planks. "But trouble follows you like a shadow. I intend to learn why."

Charlie backed away, matching Cullen's pace. The bridge narrowed his choices with every step. The river below kept its own counsel, indifferent.

"Your brother trusted the wrong man," Charlie said, choosing each word. "Crane used my name to cover his theft. When your brother pressed him, it ended badly."

"You speak as if you were there."

"No," Charlie said. "But I spoke to a man who saw the ledger. Who understood what it meant."

Cullen stopped near the center of the bridge, studying him. Snow thickened, whispering across the planks, soft against the boards, muting the sound of the river below.

"You think I followed you across half the county to listen to stories," Cullen said. "I followed you because my brother died with your name on his lips."

A gust of wind lifted the edge of Cullen's coat. His hand drifted lower, nearer the small knife at his belt.

Charlie tightened his grip on the satchel strap, feeling the weight of it press against his side. "If you kill me, the trail ends here. Crane walks free."

"Crane will not get far."

"He already has," Charlie said. "And he will keep running unless someone stops him."

Cullen shook his head slowly. "You sound too calm for a man standing over ice."

Charlie took another step back. Then another. The far end of the bridge loomed behind him. Beyond it, the slope dropped sharply into brush too dense to move through quickly, branches heavy with frost, ground uneven beneath the snow.

Cullen advanced.

Charlie looked down again at Freeman's Run. The river rushed beneath him, black water curling over white stone. The cold would be brutal. The current merciless.

But a knife would be final. He set his jaw.

"Tell me the truth," Cullen said. "One last time."

"I already have," Charlie replied.

He shifted his grip on the satchel as he spoke, buying a half-second. He pushed it higher against his shoulder, tightening the strap so it rode close beneath his coat. What little he carried that still mattered, he kept there.

Cullen lunged.

Charlie moved first. He threw himself backward over the rail.

The cold struck like a hammer. The river swallowed him whole, tearing the breath from his chest as foam and ice closed around him. The current seized him at once and dragged him downstream, slamming him against stone, rolling him under again before he could find air.

He kicked hard, fighting upward. His head broke the surface for a moment. Snow streaked overhead. The roar of water filled his ears, leaving no room for anything else.

Above him, on the bridge, Cullen leaned over the rail, looking down into the black rush below. Charlie could not tell if he was watching or waiting.

The current pulled Charlie around a bend. The bridge vanished behind him. First Fork carried him deeper into the dark, toward the long, freezing miles between Costello and the narrowing valley that led south.

Cold worked its way through him, stealing strength from his arms, his legs, his breath.

He fought to keep his head above water. He fought to stay alive.

He did not know if Cullen would follow, or if the river itself would finish what the fire had begun. But there was no turning back now.

Blowville lay ahead. And whatever waited there was closer than ever.

33

The Long Walk

November 20, 1898 - Along First Fork, South of Costello

The current carried Charlie down First Fork until the stream widened and its grip loosened. The river still had strength in it, cold and punishing, rolling him once more before pushing him into a slower bend nearly half a mile downstream. His arms burned from fighting the water. When the pull finally eased, he lunged for the bank.

His hand closed on a root slick with moss. He held fast, boots skidding on frozen mud, and dragged himself up inch by inch until he collapsed on the shore, chest heaving. Snow drifted down in light flurries. He listened hard.

No shouts carried from upstream. No footsteps broke the hush. No sign of Cullen Pratt. Only the steady push of the river answered him.

Charlie rolled onto his back and stared at the pale, empty sky. His coat was soaked through. His satchel lay beside him, heavy with water, its strap twisted where the current had pulled at it. Cold pressed in at once, sharp and purposeful. It did not wait. It moved fast, stealing strength from his hands first, then his arms, creeping inward with quiet certainty.

He knew the truth of it. If he lay still, the cold would finish what the river had started.

He forced himself upright. His hands shook violently as he unclipped the satchel and checked what remained. Some things were ruined. Paper pulped into gray paste. Cloth stiff and dark.

But his flint and tinder were still wrapped in waxed cloth, tucked deep where the water had not fully reached. When he felt them, damp at the edges but sound enough to take a spark, he let out a breath he had not realized he was holding.

He pushed himself to his feet and hauled his way up the slope toward a cluster of evergreens. Their boughs broke the wind just enough to matter. Snow gathered beneath them in thinner drifts, the ground easier to work.

He gathered fallen branches, snapping them down to size, hands clumsy and slow to answer him. He scraped away the snow with his heel until the ground showed through, dark and damp beneath the white. The flint slipped in his numb fingers.

Once. Twice.

He swore under his breath and forced his hands to steady, pressing them briefly against his sides to hold what warmth remained.

On the third strike, the tinder caught. A small flame bloomed, weak but alive. If it went out, he would not get it back.

He fed it carefully, breath measured, adding twigs one at a time until it took hold and grew into something steadier. Only then did he allow himself to sit back on his heels.

He laid his coat and boots near the heat. Steam rose from the wool in long, white ribbons, curling upward before vanishing into the cold. He did not trust it yet. He turned the coat once, then again, watching the moisture lift before letting it rest closer to the fire.

Pain flooded his fingers as warmth returned, sharp enough to make him grit his teeth. He rubbed his arms hard and leaned closer to the fire until the shaking eased into something he could manage.

Night closed in fully. The sky darkened until only the snow held any light, reflecting what little the clouds allowed. The fire crackled behind him. The river slid past in the dark, steady and indifferent.

Charlie found himself thinking not of the shed, but of Cullen's eyes in the smoke.

Men who walked into fire like that did not expect to die in it.

He reached into his coat and found the biscuit, softened from the water but still holding together. He ate it slowly, chewing longer than he needed to, as if the act itself might steady him.

The fire settled into a steady burn. The worst of the damp left his clothes. The violent shaking eased into a dull, persistent ache that settled deep in his bones. He shifted closer to the fire and curled on his side, one arm draped over his satchel, as if to keep it from drifting away in the night. Snow hissed softly into the embers.

He slept.

At first light he woke to the sound of a barred owl perched in the trees above. The fire had burned down to ash. Cold had stiffened every joint. His hands were slow to answer him, as if they belonged to someone else. He pushed himself upright and stamped his feet until feeling crept back into them, slow and reluctant.

The river ran dark beside him, ice skimming its edges, unchanged by the night. It moved on without memory.

Charlie pulled on his boots, still damp but workable, and shrugged into his coat. The wool clung cold against his skin before the first hint of warmth began to return.

He slung his half-dried satchel over his shoulder and looked south. Beyond the First Fork, the land rose and narrowed. The valley drew itself inward, funneling whatever passed through it. Somewhere down that stretch lay Blowville. Crane's trail. The ledger. The borrowed name that had nearly ended him in two towns already.

Every answer pulled him that way.

He turned from the river and followed a faint path where deer had broken the snow. It led him through brush and thin timber until it opened onto a wagon track running along the water, rutted and half frozen where wheels had passed before the last cold.

Not long after, he reached a smaller stream feeding into the First Fork.

Bailey Run.

He stopped for a moment and drew a slow breath. Smoke still clung to his clothes. His left shoulder ached with a dull, stubborn pain that had not been there before the river, jarring with each step. His ribs protested too, a quiet account of the blows taken in the current.

He tested his weight once, then again. Manageable. But he was alive. And he was farther from Cullen Pratt than he had been in weeks.

Charlie set his feet along the road that followed Bailey Run upstream. The valley tightened around him. The air sharpened. The trees stood closer together, their branches holding the cold in place. Whatever waited ahead had been waiting a long time.

He kept walking.

Part 4

Blowville

34

Arriving in Blowville

November 21 (morning), 1898 - Blowville

Snow clung to the wagon ruts along Bailey Run, turning the road pale in the early light. Charlie followed the water north until the valley opened enough to reveal Blowville, settled between the hills and already moving with the steady rhythm of winter labor.

The town was worn in places but far from failing. Smoke rose from chimneys up and down the road. The sawmill clattered at the far end of town, its belts whining through the cold. Men hauled cut hemlock to rail carts. Bark peelers shouted to one another near tall stacks of drying bark. Horses stamped at hitch posts while teamsters argued over schedules and frozen harness buckles.

Blowville was still alive. Bruised by years of work, perhaps, but awake and unyielding.

Charlie crossed into town at an even pace. People gave him the careful looks reserved for travelers who arrived in winter. Not hostile, but measuring. A pair of woodsmen leaned on their saws outside a tool shed, their talk dropping off as he passed. A woman carrying a bundle of kindling paused long enough to take his measure before continuing on. Even the children sliding on packed ice near the store quieted and drifted back toward the porch when they noticed him.

He kept his hands visible and his expression calm. A stranger could move through Blowville, but only if he made no sudden moves and asked no questions too quickly. That had not changed.

What had changed was him.

In other towns, he would have taken a game, read what he could, and moved on before anyone thought to remember him. But this time his name had arrived first.

That changed the rules.

Farther up the road, the older part of town tightened around a narrow alley running behind a line of small workshops. Most stood empty this time of year, shutters closed, doors barred against the cold. One building, however, showed a faint sign of life. A lantern glowed through a thin slit between warped boards near the back. Men slipped in and out of a side door, each pausing long enough to look both ways before disappearing inside.

Charlie slowed, watching from across the street. No sign marked the door. No noise reached the road. But the steady movement told him enough.

A pig's ear. Quiet. Unassuming. A place built to be ignored.

He stood there a moment longer than he intended. His reactions lagged a fraction behind his thoughts, as if the river had taken more from him than warmth alone. His shoulder pulled when he shifted his weight. He adjusted the satchel against it and let the discomfort settle where it would.

He waited until the moment felt right, then crossed, faintly annoyed at himself for needing the extra beat. He turned into the alley. A man leaned against the wall beside the door, hat pulled low, arms crossed over a heavy coat. His breath fogged the air in slow bursts.

"You looking for someone," the man said.

"Just a warm room," Charlie answered. "Maybe a seat."

The man studied him in silence, the kind of look that weighed not just a face, but what it carried behind it. His eyes lingered on the damp edge of Charlie's coat, the stiffness in his left side, the satchel strap drawn tighter than comfort required.

After a moment, he stepped aside.

"Keep your voice down," he said. "This room carries."

Charlie nodded once and slipped through the narrow door.

The pig's ear occupied a back room that had once held tools or lumber. Lanterns hung from nails driven into the rafters, casting a low amber light that warmed the rough pine walls. A wool blanket had been hammered over one window to block the glow from spilling into the alley. A potbelly stove smoldered in the corner, its heat reaching only partway across the room.

A narrow table claimed the center. Men with worn coats and tired eyes sat close around it. Coins lay stacked in uneven piles. Cards whispered as the dealer shuffled. Someone drank from a tin cup, the faint smell of whiskey rising through the warm air.

Conversation thinned when Charlie entered. Not suspicion exactly. Something quieter than that. Assessment. A stranger meant risk. Or information.

Charlie removed his gloves and took a seat near the end of the table. His fingers were slower than they should have been, the cold still working its way out of them. No one greeted him. No one asked him to leave. The silence itself served as permission.

The dealer nodded once and dealt him in. As the first hand unfolded, Charlie took in the room again. This pig's ear was older than the ones in Austin or Costello. Less restless. More settled into its rules. The men here knew one another. Knew debts owed and grudges held. Knew which silences mattered and which could be ignored.

He could feel the valley in it. The way Blowville held its secrets tight to the ribs.

Crane had lived here. George Ebenspecker had died not far from this ground. The ledger page bearing Charlie's name had grown out of this soil, carried forward by hands that knew exactly what they were doing.

Charlie let a small hand pass without pressing it. Then another. He was not here to win yet. Not until he understood the room well enough to know what a win would cost him.

Whatever waited for him in Blowville would not stay hidden long.

And he was done running.

35

The Pig's Ear

November 21, 1898 - Blowville

The cards moved slowly in the dim back room, their edges worn soft by years of use. Charlie sat with a small stack of coins before him, careful in every motion. He had already learned the rhythm of the place. Conversation came in murmurs too low to follow unless you leaned into it. Men touched their tin cups lightly so the room stayed calm. Even the potbelly stove in the corner burned without complaint, giving off a steady, patient heat.

The dealer, a narrow man with a narrow face, shuffled with the tired confidence of someone who had handled more hands than he could remember. He looked at Charlie only as much as the game required, no more, no less.

Charlie won small pots, just enough to keep his seat without drawing notice. The locals played with a sober patience. Their tells were faint. A twitch at the edge of a beard. A thumb worrying a card's corner. A knee that bounced only when a man found himself deeper than he had planned.

A lumberman across from him took a sip from his cup and studied Charlie with quiet curiosity.

"You not from around here," he said.

"Just arrived," Charlie answered.

"And staying where," the lumberman asked. The question came softly, more observation than challenge.

Charlie hesitated. “Nowhere yet. Came through late. Figured I would find something in the morning.”

The lumberman lifted his brows and returned his attention to the table, but the exchange had carried. At the far end, an older man with thinning hair and a coat worn shiny at the elbows leaned back in his chair. He scratched at his jaw and spoke without lifting his eyes from his cards.

“I got a storeroom over my shop,” he said. “Old place on the north road. Used to keep tools there, but most of it moved out last winter. There’s a cot. Window looks toward the creek. Cold mornings, but it holds.”

The dealer paused mid-shuffle. The room went a shade quieter.

Charlie looked toward the man. “What will it cost.”

“Three bits a day,” the man said. “You sweep the steps when they need it and keep to yourself.”

Charlie considered him, then nodded. It was fair. More than fair, given how Blowville weighed strangers.

“Name’s Barnes,” the older man added, turning a card slowly between his fingers. “Ask around and you’ll find the place.”

“I appreciate it,” Charlie said.

Barnes shrugged. “Town fills quick once winter settles. Better to have a roof early.”

The dealer resumed shuffling. The next hand fell into place.

Charlie played a few more rounds, careful as ever. When the final hand ended, the men drifted out into the alley one by one, each returning to whatever corners of Blowville carried them through the season.

Charlie lingered only a moment. He breathed in the odd warmth of the room, the smell of pine smoke and damp wool, the low hum of a place that kept its own counsel. The pig’s ear felt older than the town around it, like something left standing because no one quite dared remove it.

Outside, frost already filmed the alley. The lookout nodded once as Charlie passed.

The main road lay quiet, sleepers behind drawn curtains. Only the mill house lantern, kept low for the night watch, flickered in the distance. Charlie found the north road and followed it until Barnes's shop came into view. The building stood firm against the dark, roof pitched steep, windows shuttered tight. A narrow stair ran up the side to a small landing.

Charlie climbed it and found the key exactly where Barnes had said, tucked beneath a loose board beside the door.

The room above the shop was plain but sound. A cot against one wall. A dry sink. A small stove with a short run of pipe. No comfort, but shelter enough.

Charlie set down his satchel and stood by the window for a moment, looking toward the creek. Bailey Run glimmered faintly between the dark trees.

This town carried a watchfulness that reminded him of Costello, but deeper and more settled. Blowville was not trying to frighten him. It was trying to decide what he was worth.

Whatever waited here would not stay hidden long.

36

Watched

November 22, 1898 - Blowville

Charlie woke before dawn to the sound of the creek moving beneath thin ice. Bailey Run murmured like someone speaking from the far end of a long hallway. The room above Barnes's shop was cold enough that his breath showed with every exhale.

He dressed slowly, working stiffness from his hands and shoulders. The ache lingered, dull and persistent, a reminder of the river and the night it had taken from him. When he stepped outside, the sky was still purple with early light. Any glow along the road came not from street lamps but from a few houses where early risers had set lanterns in windows, or from the faint orange flicker drifting from the sawmill, where the night watch kept their fire banked low.

Blowville was already stirring.

Woodsmen walked toward the mill yard in pairs, collars pulled high, tools slung over their shoulders. Bark peelers moved together down the road, boots crunching over frost. Their voices stayed low, but nearly every one of them gave Charlie a careful look as he passed.

A stranger in winter always drew attention. But here the attention felt narrower, more exact. Not curiosity so much as recognition. As if Blowville had been expecting someone, and Charlie fit the outline closely enough to trouble them.

He headed toward the center of town and stopped at Mohan General Store, one of the few places already open. A thin plume of steam drifted from a kettle near the doorway. The woman behind the counter greeted him politely, but her eyes followed him across the room, visible in the curved reflection of a glass jar she polished.

Two men seated near the back quieted the moment he entered. One stirred his coffee without looking up. The other met Charlie's eyes openly, held them a second longer than necessary, then returned his attention to his cup as though nothing had happened.

Charlie drank his coffee, ate his biscuit, and stepped back into the cold.

Across the road, the lookout from the pig's ear stood near the harness shop, bent over a length of leather as if repairing a strap. His hands moved steadily, but his eyes lifted the moment Charlie came into view. He did not speak. He only watched.

Charlie kept walking.

He paused at the notice board beside the post office. New winter postings had been tacked over older ones, paper layered on paper. Some sheets had corners torn away. One carried a name that had been scratched out with a sharp point, gouged hard enough to leave the wood scarred beneath.

A boy came out of the post office with an armful of letters. He stopped short when he saw Charlie, then turned and hurried off in the opposite direction.

Charlie left the board and followed the road toward the mill yard. Steam rolled from the mill roof. The saws tore through hemlock with a steady roar. Men shouted measurements over the noise of cutting. Honest sound. The kind that usually pushed worry aside.

But even here, heads turned.

A foreman paused long enough to take Charlie's measure before moving on. A cluster of woodsmen near the loading area fell quiet as he passed, their conversation resuming only after he was several paces beyond them.

Charlie crossed the yard and followed the north road until the forest pressed closer. From there he could see the roofline of the Fee Brothers mill house rising beyond a low ridge. The building was large and old, built when the town believed its best years lay ahead. The porch stood empty. Curtains were drawn tight. The place held a stillness that made Charlie keep to the road.

By midday he circled back toward the center of Blowville. He had learned nothing certain. Only that the town was paying attention.

Near the butcher's shop, two men spoke in low voices.

"That the fellow," one asked.

"Could be," the other replied. "Looks close enough."

Neither said more. They watched him walk on.

The sky clouded early, promising snow. Charlie returned to Barnes's shop and climbed the narrow stairs to his room. He stood by the window, looking down at the road as the light thinned.

Men passed in ones and twos. Some carried tools. Some hauled bundles of wood. A few looked up toward his window without hiding it. Others kept their faces forward, casting a glance only when they thought he was not watching.

Blowville was watching. And not by chance.

Charlie sat on the edge of the cot, rubbing warmth back into his hands, feeling the delay in his movements, the faint hesitation that still followed thought.

He had come searching for Crane. For George Ebenspecker's truth. For the reason his own name had traveled ahead of him into this valley.

Blowville knew pieces of that truth. And Blowville was waiting.

37

Sarah Ebenspecker

November 22 (evening), 1898 - Blowville

The afternoon light had thinned to a gray wash by the time Charlie left Barnes's shop again. Snow threatened but had not yet fallen. The road through the center of Blowville carried the slow, steady movement of men finishing their shifts. A few stores remained open. Most homes were already drawing curtains against the cold.

Charlie kept his hands in his coat pockets as he walked, letting his thoughts narrow. Crane. Always Crane. Whatever had begun in Galeton and chased him through Austin and Costello had roots here, tangled deep in this valley. Blowville did not feel like a place a man passed through by accident.

He turned toward Bailey Run, thinking a walk might settle his head, when he noticed a figure standing near the bridge.

A woman stood with her hands resting on the rail, her coat drawn close at the throat. She did not look away when he saw her. She looked straight at him, as though she had already decided who he was.

Charlie slowed.

She pushed off the rail and crossed the road toward him. Her boots moved without hurry. Her eyes held his in a quiet, unwavering study. She was beautiful in a way that made people temper their voices, but nothing about her suggested softness. Her presence felt honed, steadied by something sharpened through use.

"You are Charles Randall," she said.

It was not a question.

Charlie felt the familiar tightening beneath his ribs. Not the jolt of immediate danger, but the weight of something considered and deliberate. "Who told you that," he asked.

"No one needed to," she said. "You walk like a man who has been followed through half the county. And Blowville notices men like that."

He did not look away. "And you are."

"Sarah Ebenspecker."

The name settled between them. He had heard it spoken quietly in more than one town. A name tied to a death. A name that led back to Crane.

Charlie straightened a fraction. "I heard about your father."

Most people softened at the mention of grief. Sarah did not. Her posture held. Her gaze did not waver. "People say many things about my father," she said. "Few of them are true."

Charlie waited. Snow began to drift down, thin flakes passing between them.

"I saw you last night," she continued. "At the pig's ear behind the workshops."

He nodded once. "I did not see you."

"You were not meant to." She stepped closer, close enough that he could see the resolve set behind her eyes. "I watch newcomers. Especially those who carry a name someone else used when my father died."

The ground shifted under him, slow but unmistakable. "Who used my name."

"Crane."

She said it plainly. No weight added. No hesitation.

Charlie glanced past her toward the mill house in the distance, its windows dark even at this hour. "I never met him," he said. "Not once."

Sarah studied him again, longer this time, as if testing the shape of his words against what she already knew. "Maybe not," she said at last. "But his choices have a way of following you."

She reached into her coat and withdrew a folded scrap of paper. The edges were worn soft from handling. She did not open it. She held it between them, enough to make its presence felt.

"I have something of Crane's," she said. "He gave it to me in October. It has your name on it."

The cold pressed harder against Charlie's chest. "Why show me."

"Because I have been waiting for you," Sarah said. "And because whatever Crane set in motion is not finished with either of us."

The snow thickened. The wind shifted along the run, lifting her coat slightly before it settled again.

Sarah slipped the paper back into her pocket and stepped away. "You should find a warm place," she said. "It will be dark soon, and this town grows smaller at night."

He watched her cross the bridge, her figure steady against the falling snow, until she disappeared down the path that followed the run.

Charlie remained where he was, the cold creeping through his boots, uncertain whether the meeting had brought him closer to answers or only widened the space around them.

But one thing was clear.

Sarah Ebenspecker had been looking for him. And whatever she carried in that folded scrap was about to pull him deeper into Blowville than he had ever intended to go.

38

Sarah's Story

November 23 (morning), 1898 - Blowville

Charlie found her again the next morning. Or perhaps she found him. It was hard to tell.

He had left Barnes's shop to walk the edge of town, hoping the cold would settle his thoughts, when he saw her standing near the footbridge that crossed Bailey Run. Her hands were tucked into her coat sleeves, her attention fixed on the water sliding beneath a skin of ice.

She did not turn when he approached. She spoke as if she had been expecting him.

"You have questions," she said.

He stopped beside her. Frost clung to the rail, whitening the wood. The morning sun had not yet reached the valley floor.

"Your father's name keeps coming up," Charlie said. "I want to understand why."

Sarah breathed out slowly, the breath lifting in a pale plume. "My father worked in the woods. Same as most men here. He kept to himself. Paid what he owed. Helped when help was needed. Nothing about him drew attention."

She traced a finger along the iced rail, leaving a narrow line behind. "But he noticed things. Small things. Who carried extra scrip through town. Why the paymaster's tallies never matched what men said they were owed. Why strangers came through Blowville after dark and did not stay long."

Charlie listened. He did not interrupt.

"One morning, in the fall of ninety-five, they found him in the creek north of town, near the bend." Her voice stayed even, but every word carried weight. "They said he had been drinking at the pig's ear the night before. That he slipped and struck his head on a rock."

"And you did not believe it," Charlie said.

Sarah turned her eyes to him for the first time. They were steady, sharp, and unsparing. "My father did not drink enough to stumble. And the back of his skull was split open. Clean. Straight. A fall in shallow water does not do that."

Charlie nodded. He had heard this shape of lie before. It always came dressed as certainty.

"I came to Blowville a couple years later," Sarah said. "I needed answers no one in my own town would give me. Work was the simplest way to stay close to the people who might know something, so I took a position in Terrence Fee's house. Not for the wages. For what men said when they thought no one was listening. I learned more sweeping floors than I ever did reading county records."

"And Crane," Charlie said.

Sarah looked away toward the trees lining the run. Her jaw tightened slightly. "He came often. Trusted by Fee. Always watchful. Always listening. He was not unkind to me. But he carried something heavy. Something he did not speak aloud."

Charlie waited.

"Crane knew about my father," she continued. "Not everything. Enough to make me wonder how close he stood to it. Sometimes he seemed ready to tell me something important. Other times he shut down, as if a door had closed inside him."

She reached into her coat and touched the pocket where the folded scrap rested, though she did not remove it.

"He gave me that paper in October," she said. "Told me to hide it. Told me not to show it unless someone came asking for him."

"Someone like me," Charlie said.

Her eyes returned to his. "Someone carrying your name."

Silence settled between them. The creek murmured under the ice. A raven called once from the trees and went quiet again.

"You trusted him," Charlie said.

Sarah did not answer right away. When she did, her voice had softened, though her posture did not. "I thought I did. It is harder now to tell what was real and what he kept from me. Crane wanted something. Something dangerous. And whatever it was, it swallowed him whole."

Charlie studied her. Her calm was not distance. It was control. Grief held tight and sharpened rather than broken.

"Why tell me all this," he asked.

"Because you cannot outrun what Crane started," she said. "And neither can I."

She stepped back from the rail. Snow crunched under her boots.

"I will show you the page tomorrow," she said. "You will understand why he wrote your name. But the truth does not end with that scrap of paper. It begins there."

She turned and walked toward the center of town, her stride measured, her purpose clear.

When she was gone, Charlie looked down at the water running beneath the ice, feeling the pull of something deeper than rumor or coincidence.

Whatever Crane had set in motion had already entwined their lives.

And Blowville was the only place where it could be unraveled.

39

Crane's Shadow

November 23 (afternoon), 1898 - Blowville

Charlie found work for his hands that morning to keep his thoughts from closing in. Barnes had asked him to sweep the shop steps and split a little wood, and Charlie took the chores without complaint. The motions steadied him. The scrape of broom on plank. The dull thud of axe into grain. For a time, it was enough.

By midday the questions returned, circling like ravens above a carcass.

Crane. Sarah. The ledger. His own name, written by a man he had never met.

In the afternoon, Charlie walked the road toward Bailey Run again. He did not expect to find Sarah there, but she stood near the bend in the creek as if she had been waiting since dawn.

"You came," she said.

"You expected I would."

A faint smile touched her mouth. "Crane has a way of drawing people after him, even when he is gone."

Charlie stepped beside her. Frost rimed the stones along the bank. Where the current slowed, a thin skin of ice cracked and drifted apart.

"What was he like," Charlie asked. "Before everything changed."

Sarah considered the question before answering. "Different, at first. Quiet, but not withdrawn. He noticed things. A broken latch. A missing tool. A stranger with mud on only one boot. He did not speak much, but he saw everything."

"And later."

"Later he looked over his shoulder more than he looked ahead." She pulled her coat tighter. "He grew restless. Distracted. Some mornings he arrived at Fee's house with leaves in his hair, his clothes damp, as if he had been walking the woods all night. One day his eyes were bright. The next they were hollow."

"Someone was pressing him," Charlie said.

Sarah nodded. "Fee relied on him. Trusted him with errands no one else handled. Money. Messages. Conversations that happened after dark in the front room. Crane never repeated a word of it, but it stayed with him. Some nights he could not hide that."

"Did he ever tell you what he was afraid of," Charlie asked.

"Not plainly." Sarah watched the water for a long moment. "But once, in early October, he asked me something strange. He asked if I ever felt watched in the woods. Not followed. Watched. As if the trees noticed you before you noticed them."

Charlie frowned. "And you told him."

"I told him the woods have always watched us. Every logger knows that feeling." She turned to him. "But Crane meant something else. Something he hesitant to give a name to."

A chill ran through Charlie that had nothing to do with the cold. He had walked forests his whole life. Some held silence. Some held threat. Blowville's woods held something that pressed inward.

"After that," Sarah said, "Crane began carrying a ledger. Not a full book. Just a handful of pages torn from somewhere else. He kept them hidden in his coat. Fee never asked. Or if he did, Crane never answered."

"The page you have," Charlie said.

She touched her pocket. "He tore it from that set. Gave it to me and told me to keep it safe."

Charlie waited. “Do you think he is dead.”

“I think the woods do not always return what enters them,” she said. “And Crane knew that.”

The wind shifted. Bare branches rattled overhead. Snow brushed the air again, thin flakes catching on Sarah’s coat.

She stepped away from the bank. “I will show you the page soon. But not here. Not where anyone might see. Blowville listens in ways people forget.”

Charlie nodded. “Tonight.”

“Tonight,” she agreed. “At my boarding room. After the mill whistle. I will leave a lamp in the window.”

She turned to go, boots cracking the frozen path.

Before she moved out of earshot, she said, “Whatever Crane wrote, he meant for you to understand it. Be ready for that.”

Then she disappeared up the road, leaving Charlie alone with the sense that Crane’s shadow had been waiting for him long before he ever set foot in Blowville.

* * *

Charlie remained by the creek after Sarah was gone. The cold pressed harder then, as if the valley had held its breath until she finished speaking. The water slid on, dark and patient.

By late afternoon he walked toward the back of the workshop where the pig’s ear kept its door half-open to the quiet world outside. The lantern within cast a thin amber glow, enough to guide those who knew the way without drawing the law’s eye.

Charlie paused at the threshold and let the warmth settle over him as he stepped inside. The smell of pine smoke, damp wool, cheap whiskey, and worn felt steadied him more than he expected.

A few men nodded in his direction. Not welcome, not warning. Simply recognition. A place like this measured newcomers quickly, and Charlie had not given it reason to take offense.

The stove crackled. Woodsmen played cards at the far table. The dealer from Charlie's first night was there, shuffling without looking down, letting the rhythm of the cards set the room's pace.

Charlie took a seat and bought in modestly. Enough to matter. Not enough to draw comment. The cards came slow. He won small. Lost small. Each hand gave him a little space to think.

Crane walking the woods. Crane carrying pages he would not explain. Crane writing Charlie Randall's name on something meant to stay hidden.

Sarah's voice returned with every turn of the cards. Crane drew people after him even when he was gone.

The dealer slid a pot toward him. Charlie raked the coins in quietly, eyes on the scarred tabletop.

"You play careful," a woodsman across from him said.

Charlie gave a slight nod. "Careful keeps me in the chair."

The woodsman smirked and dealt again.

Charlie stayed another hour. Long enough for the weight of Sarah's words to settle. Not long enough to invite notice. When he finally pushed back from the table, the dealer glanced at him in a way that might have been approval or warning. Hard to tell.

Outside, night had fully come. The cold thickened the air. Charlie's breath rose pale as he stepped into the alley. Lanterns glimmered across the hollow, scattered points of light holding back the dark.

He walked toward Barnes's shop with his collar pulled high. Near the road's end, he looked up toward the ridge where Sarah's boarding house stood among the clustered buildings.

Tonight, she had said. After the whistle. A lamp in the window.

Answers close enough to reach. Danger close enough to feel.

Behind Barnes's shop, Charlie climbed the steps and went inside, readying himself for whatever waited in that lamplit room.

40

The Page in the Lamplight

November 23 (night), 1898 - Blowville

Snow whispered against the dark as Charlie climbed the narrow path toward the ridge. The town lay quiet below him, lanterns dimmed, sawdust heaps striped pale under the moon. Only the faint hum of the mill carried upward, drifting across the hill like a tired breath.

A single lamp burned in the upstairs window of the boarding house Sarah shared with two seamstresses. It was not bright. Just enough to mark the place she meant him to find.

Charlie paused at the porch steps and brushed the cold from his coat. He knocked once. The door opened before his hand fell back to his side.

Sarah stood there wrapped in a wool shawl, her face composed except for the tension held in her eyes. She stepped aside and motioned him in without a word.

The house smelled of drying herbs and woodsmoke. A kettle hissed faintly on the stove. Sarah led him to a small front room furnished with a rocking chair, a writing table, and the lamp she had promised, turned low so the glass barely glowed.

"Sit," she said.

Charlie took the chair nearest the table. He kept his hat on his knee, his hands steady though something in Sarah's stillness warned him that what followed would not be easily undone.

She crossed to the table and slid open the drawer. From it she removed a folded paper, its edges softened by repeated handling. She did not look at him as she brought it over. She sat across from him but angled slightly away, as if even now the truth carried weight enough to bruise.

"This is what Crane gave me," she said quietly. "The last night I saw him. Back in October."

She set the paper between them.

Charlie hesitated. "You are certain you want to show me this."

"You came here for answers," she said. "So did I." She touched the folded sheet with the back of her fingers. "Whatever is written there started both of our roads."

Charlie unfolded it carefully.

It was a ledger page, torn clean from a larger book. Columns ruled by hand. Entries written with careful precision. At first he saw only dates and sums. Then his eyes caught the line at the center.

CHARLES RANDALL — PAID IN FULL

The ink had faded, but not enough to blur the lie.

Something tightened behind Charlie's ribs. He read it again, slower this time, though he already knew what it said.

"This is not mine," he said. "I never saw this page. Never earned this money. Never signed for it."

"I know," Sarah said. Her voice was clipped, brittle.

"You sound certain."

"I am." She tapped the page once. "Crane had a way of looking honest. He could stand in front of you and make you believe he meant well. I believed him." Her mouth tightened. "I do not anymore."

She drew a slow breath, steadying herself.

"He told me he had used a name that was not his to gain footing in something larger than himself. He said it would make sense once he proved his worth." Her eyes hardened. "He never said whose name he borrowed."

Charlie folded the page with care. "You think there are more entries like this."

"I know there are."

"And whatever he was involved in," Charlie said, "that is what took him."

Sarah leaned back, her gaze cutting toward the window where snow drifted past like sifted ash. "Crane was not killed by the woods or whatever he feared in them. Men did this. The kind who smile in daylight and cut throats in the dark."

Charlie let the silence hold before asking, "You think you know who."

She nodded once. "Barclay."

Charlie frowned. "I do not know the name."

"You would not," she said. "Joseph Barclay runs the freight sheds and a pig's ear tucked behind them. He keeps a clean office for the public and a dirty business beneath it. Debt collections. Favors. Illegal drink. And theft moving quietly through the pig's ears."

Charlie absorbed that. "You think Crane worked for him."

"I think Crane wanted to," Sarah said. Her hands folded together, knuckles whitening. "Barclay rewards loyalty with money. He rewards ambition with blood. Crane thought he could rise under him. He was wrong."

Charlie exhaled slowly. "So Barclay holds the rest of this ledger. And he knows my name is written into his business."

"Yes."

"And he will not like that I am in town."

"No." Sarah's voice carried no doubt. "He will not."

Charlie rose, hat in hand, the shapes of danger rearranging themselves in his mind. "Then tomorrow we start with Barclay."

Sarah stood as well. The lamplight cast shallow shadows across her face, softening nothing.

"No," she said. "Tomorrow we start with the truth. Barclay comes after."

Charlie paused. "You trust me with this."

"I do not know yet," she said honestly. "But I trust what this page means. Crane lied to both of us. He used you. He used me. And someone profited from it."

She folded the ledger page carefully, as though closing a wound.

Charlie nodded. "Tomorrow, then."

Sarah turned down the lamp, leaving the room washed in pale moonlight. Charlie stepped toward the door, but before he reached it she spoke again, quieter now.

"Crane was not the man I wanted him to be," she said. "But I will see the men who made him into what he became."

Charlie met her eyes. There was no affection there. No grief either. Only resolve.

He stepped out into the night, snow gathering at his feet, the cold cutting clean across his face.

Behind him, Sarah stood in the doorway a moment longer before closing it, the folded ledger page held tight in her hand.

Tomorrow had already begun.

41

Charlie's Realization

November 23 (night), 1898 - Blowville

Snow thickened as Charlie made his way down from the ridge, the narrow path blurring behind him under a steady drift. Blowville lay muted below, half-swallowed by night. Chimneys breathed thin trails into the cold air. Windows glowed faintly, amber squares set deep in shadow.

He kept his stride even and let the cold settle his thoughts.

Sarah had stood in the doorway as he left, one hand closed around the folded ledger page as though it might slip away if she loosened her grip. He remembered the look in her eyes. Not sorrow. Not confusion. Something harder. Something resolved. It told him she would not set that page aside until she was ready to see the end of it.

Crane had used his name.

That truth traveled with him through the falling snow. Not a rumor passed in a pig's ear. Not a mistake made in drink. A choice. Deliberate. Written in Crane's own hand to hide his steps and push danger onto someone else.

Charlie reached Barnes's shop and let himself inside. The room was cold and narrow, the air still. He lit the stove, fed it a strip of kindling, and waited for the flame to catch. Heat came slowly, bringing with it the faint metallic scent of warming iron.

He sat on the edge of the cot with his elbows braced on his knees.

Crane had been ambitious, Sarah had said. Hungry for something Blowville never gave freely. Ambition in towns like this drew men toward the wrong fires. It promised shortcuts where none existed.

Barclay.

Charlie had never heard the name until tonight, but the way Sarah spoke it left no doubt. A man who moved freight and money and fear in equal measure. A man allowed to stand because pushing him down would cost too much. A man who rewarded loyalty and punished doubt without warning.

And Crane had wanted to matter to him.

Charlie leaned back against the wall and closed his eyes. The ledger page rose in his mind with unwanted clarity. Not the drawer she took it from or the way she folded it again. Just the paper itself. Just the words set down in ink.

Paid in full.

Paid for what. Paid by whom. And how many men had accepted that line without asking what it cost.

Trouble like this did not fade on its own. It followed. It settled into a man's shadow and waited.

Charlie rubbed a hand along his jaw. He knew how easily a name could become a burden. He had spent years stepping around old rumors, avoiding places where people thought they recognized him. But this was different. This was crafted. Intentional. Crane had placed his name where it did not belong and walked away from the consequences.

Now those consequences were waiting here.

He thought again of Sarah. Her voice steady, sharpened by restraint. The bitterness that surfaced each time she spoke Crane's name. She had shown him the page not out of trust, but out of necessity. She needed someone willing to stand where she could not stand alone. Charlie understood that. He respected it.

He lay back on the cot, boots set neatly beside it, coat still on. The stove worked against the cold, pushing shadows toward the corners of the room.

Tomorrow they would begin. She had said as much. Charlie could already feel the path narrowing, choices drawing tight around him. Barclay. The scrip. The men who had followed Crane until they did not anymore.

Sleep came slowly. Names carried weight. Ledger ink remembered what men wished forgotten. Some burdens sank deeper than snow.

When Charlie finally closed his eyes, his mind did not quiet.

He understood then that he had stopped running the moment Sarah placed that page in the lamplight.

42

Sarah's Request

November 24 (morning), 1898 - Blowville

Morning came thin and gray, the kind of light that barely reached the valley before slipping behind the ridgeline again. Charlie woke stiff from the cold and from thoughts that had not left him even in sleep. The stove had gone dead sometime in the night, leaving the room coated in a brittle chill.

He coaxed the fire back to life, washed his face in a tin basin, and stepped outside. Snow had hardened overnight into a crust that cracked under his boots. The sky looked ready to break open again.

Down the slope, the mill whistle groaned low, calling men toward their work. Charlie followed the beaten path toward the ridge where Sarah boarded. Smoke curled from the chimney there, thin and wavering against the pale sky.

She was already outside, brushing snow from the porch rail. She did not look surprised to see him. She did not look fully rested either.

"Cold morning," he said.

She nodded once. "Come inside."

The sitting room held a little warmth, though not enough to soften the air completely. Sarah closed the door behind him and crossed to the small table near the window. The ledger page lay there, unfolded, its corner held down by a smooth river stone.

Charlie did not reach for it. Neither did she.

"We need to find where it came from," Sarah said.

Charlie remained standing. "You said Crane disappeared in October. Whatever he was involved in, it turned on him around then."

"Yes." Her eyes stayed on the page. "But not by chance. Someone pushed him out. Someone with enough pull to make a man vanish without explanation."

"Barclay," Charlie said.

Her jaw tightened. "He is the one I can see clearly. But he is not alone. Men do not forge ledgers for themselves. There is someone behind the numbers. Someone who signs the pay."

"The paymaster."

"Most likely."

Charlie considered that. "So where do we begin."

Sarah lifted the page, folded it with careful precision, and slipped it inside her coat. "We begin where Crane began. His meeting place."

"Where is that."

She hesitated, then met his eyes. "South of town. Off the timber road. A clearing he visited more than he should have." Something uneasy passed through her expression. "He went there when he did not want Fee to see him. Or anyone else."

Charlie nodded. "You have been there."

"Once." She adjusted the shawl around her shoulders. "He made it sound harmless. A place to think. I know now it was where he conducted business. Quiet exchanges. The kind men hide once they have stepped too far into something they cannot control."

She moved toward the door.

"If we are going to follow his trail," she said, "it begins there."

Charlie studied her face. She was different this morning. Harder. The bitterness he had heard the night before had settled into something steadier. Resolve shaped by anger, but sharpened by clarity.

"You certain you want to walk back into whatever he left behind," he asked.

"I want the truth," she said. She opened the door and let the cold rush in. "Whatever shape it takes."

Charlie reached for his coat. "Then lead the way."

They stepped outside into the sharp morning. Snow shifted beneath their boots as they turned south. Sarah kept the folded page close against her chest.

Whatever Crane had started in this valley, they were moving straight toward it.

43

The Clearing in the Woods

November 24 (late morning), 1898 - North of Blowville

The timber road narrowed quickly once they left the last of Blowville behind. Snow lay deeper here, undisturbed except for faint deer tracks and the long drag marks left by sled runners hauling logs earlier in the season. The trees pressed closer the farther they walked, branches bent low beneath the weight of winter.

Sarah walked ahead with a certainty that told Charlie she had learned every turn of this path long ago. She spoke little, only lifting a hand once at a fork where fresher tracks veered right.

“We go left,” she said.

Charlie followed, boots sinking into the snow. The cold bit at his face, but the quiet of the woods settled something in him. Towns held lies too tightly. Forests let them surface.

They walked another quarter hour before Sarah slowed. The trees opened into a shallow hollow ringed by hemlock and birch. Even beneath snow, the place showed signs of disturbance. Old footprints pressed thin. A fire pit sunken into the ground. Broken branches stacked with a care too deliberate to be accidental.

“This was it,” Sarah said softly.

Charlie stepped into the clearing, crouching near the fire pit. Beneath the crust of snow, blackened stones held the remains of old ash.

“When was the last time he came here,” Charlie asked.

"October," she said. "The week before he gave me the page."

Charlie brushed snow away near the edge of the pit. Something pale caught against his glove. He eased it free. The paper tore slightly in his hand, brittle with weather, but faint ink clung to one corner.

"Ledger scrap," he said. "Same hand. Same columns."

Sarah stepped closer, eyes narrowing as she studied it. "He burned the rest."

"Not well enough," Charlie said, gesturing to the charred remains. "Enough to hide it from anyone not looking too hard."

She turned slowly, scanning the hollow as if the ground itself might speak. "He met someone here. I know he did. He said Blowville watched him too closely. Said he needed daylight and quiet, somewhere no one could overhear."

"Did he ever say who," Charlie asked.

"No." Her voice tightened. "He wanted to impress someone. Prove he could be more than Fee's shadow. More than a man haunted by things he would not name."

Charlie circled the clearing. Near a half-buried stump, the snow sloped wrong. He kicked away the top layer, then knelt and brushed the rest aside with his bare hand.

Beneath it lay a small pile of half-burned scrip. The edges curled and blackened. The center still showed faint traces of Goodyear print.

Sarah drew in a sharp breath. "He kept some."

"Or someone left it here for him," Charlie said.

She knelt beside the pile, gloved fingers hovering but not touching. "He told me he was saving money," she said quietly. "Said he had plans. A future."

For an instant, the clearing tilted. Sarah steadied herself with a hand against the stump, angry not at Crane yet, but at herself for how easily she had wanted to believe him. "He never trusted me enough to tell me any of this."

Charlie straightened. "A man caught between fear and ambition does not trust easily. Sometimes not at all."

Sarah stood, shoulders squaring. "Barclay's men used this place. I can feel it. Crane wanted in. He thought he could manage it."

"He was wrong," Charlie said.

She looked toward the path leading back to town. "If Barclay knew about this clearing, he may have already taken what mattered."

Charlie brushed snow from his coat. "This confirms it. He was tied to stolen scrip. Deep enough to leave traces behind."

"And he wrote your name to do it."

They stood in silence, the wind threading through the trees, the clearing breathing around them.

"There is another place," Sarah said at last. "A shed near the freight house. Crane mentioned it once. Said Barclay kept ledgers there he did not want seen."

Charlie nodded. "Then that's where we go next."

Sarah turned toward the path back to town. The ledger scraps remained behind, dark flecks against the snow.

The forest closed gently around them as they walked away. Whatever Crane had left in that clearing no longer belonged to him.

It belonged to whoever followed.

And Charlie and Sarah had only begun.

44

Crane's Rise and Fall

November 24 (midday), 1898 - Blowville

They reached the edge of town near midday, boots crusted with snow, the cold clinging to their coats like a second skin. Sarah stopped beside a split-rail fence overlooking the freight yard below. Logs were stacked in careful rows. Men moved between the sheds like dark figures cut from the white ground.

She said nothing at first. Her eyes traced the yard's neat geometry, the ordered movement, the quiet authority of a place that handled other men's labor and money. Charlie let the silence stand.

"Crane wanted to be seen," she said at last. "He acted like he had no use for the mills, the freight, the men who kept the books. But he watched them. Studied them."

Charlie rested a hand against the fence. "He wanted out from under Fee."

Sarah nodded. "Fee was strong once. People feared him. Respected him. But the last year or so his mind slipped. He stopped watching the ledgers. Stopped watching Crane."

Charlie remembered the way she had spoken of Fee before. A man whose presence had kept certain lies from growing too bold. "Crane saw the opening."

"Yes. And he took it." She lifted her chin toward the largest shed near the tracks. "That one. Barclay works out of there. Crane spent more time near it once Fee stopped paying attention."

Charlie studied the building. Plain boards. Three windows. A freight door left half open. Nothing about it announced danger. Places like that never did.

"He was ambitious," Charlie said. "But ambition without direction turns into something else."

Sarah's expression tightened. "Ambition mixed with fear. That's what Crane carried. Fear of Fee losing his grip. Fear of being forgotten. Fear of whatever he met in those woods." She shook her head once. "Fear makes a man reckless."

Charlie weighed that. "So he used my name to give himself a step up."

"Yes. A drifter with no ties. Easy to blame if something went wrong." Her mouth set. "He told me once people remembered faces better than names. Said if trouble came, no one would look for the man who signed the book."

Charlie breathed out slowly. "And when Barclay saw Crane couldn't hold what he'd taken…"

"He cut him loose." There was no surprise in her voice, only the confirmation of something she had already accepted. "Barclay doesn't tolerate failure. Or hesitation. Or regret."

Sarah turned her gaze toward the woods beyond the yard, her breath rising in pale curls. "I wanted to believe Crane died trying to fix something. That he made mistakes but wasn't cruel at heart." She looked back at the sheds. "But he wasn't innocent. Not blind. Not confused. He climbed toward something he thought would make him strong."

"And it killed him," Charlie said.

"No," she replied quietly. "The men behind the scrip killed him. And Crane's choices made it easy."

For a moment the only sounds were distant hammer blows from the mill and the low rumble of a handcart along the tracks. Charlie watched her and saw not grief but clarity settling into her posture, straightening her where sorrow once had weight.

"You said this morning we start with the truth," he said. "This looks like part of it."

She nodded. "Crane was rising too fast. Forging entries. Carrying scrip. Meeting men in the woods. And then…"

"He fell," Charlie said.

Sarah met his eyes. "Now we find out who pushed him."

Charlie looked again at the freight shed. "You think Barclay still keeps the ledgers there."

"If he does, they won't be easy to reach," she said. "He's careful."

Charlie stepped away from the fence, brushing snow from his gloves. "Careful men leave traces. They have to."

Sarah moved beside him. "Then we start looking."

They turned back toward town, toward the tightening knot of streets, the general stores, the chimneys breathing smoke into the low sky. Behind them, the freight shed remained quiet and unremarkable.

But Charlie felt its weight. The shape of the truth was beginning to hold. Crane had reached for power. Someone had offered it. Someone had taken it back.

And Charlie Randall, without choosing any of it, had been written into the center of the account.

45

Threats in the Dark

November 24 (evening), 1898 - Blowville

The snow eased as afternoon thinned into a cold, pale light. Charlie and Sarah followed the timber road back toward Blowville, boots cracking through the crust forming atop the morning's snowfall. From a distance the town looked unchanged. Smoke lifted from chimneys. The mill kept its steady rhythm. Children ran along packed paths, their laughter sharp in the cold air.

But people watched them now.

A logger carrying an axe slowed as they passed, his eyes moving from Sarah to Charlie before sliding away a beat too late. Two bark peelers muttered near a wagon and fell silent when Sarah glanced their way. At the edge of the freight yard, a man leaning against a crate adjusted his gloves without need, his attention fixed on them until they were well past.

Sarah kept her voice low. "They know we were out there."

Charlie did not answer, but the tightness in his chest said the same thing.

They paused near Mohan General Store. Sarah said she needed to return to the boarding house but would meet him again at dusk. Before she turned away, she touched his arm once and nodded toward the freight yard.

"You should know," she said. "There's another pig's ear in town. Not the quiet one you've been using."

Charlie's brow lifted. "Where."

"Behind the freight shed. Long, low building. No windows." Her voice stayed steady, but the edge beneath it was sharp. "Barclay's place."

Charlie looked again toward the yard. "Barclay runs a pig's ear."

"He runs anything tied to money moving through Blowville," she said. "That's where the drinking and gambling go past tolerance. Where men go when they want trouble no one asks about later."

"And Crane wanted to rise in that crowd."

Sarah's expression confirmed it.

She took the ridge path up toward the boarding house, leaving Charlie at the split in the road with fewer choices than before. He stepped onto Mohan's porch, bought a tin of coffee, and watched the town from the shallow shelter.

Now that he knew where Barclay's pig's ear sat, the freight shed made more sense. A careful placement. Shielded from the road. Visible only to those who already knew where to look.

Charlie finished the coffee and headed back toward Barnes's storeroom. Near the feed shed, the same man he had noticed earlier appeared again, studying a stack of lumber with too much care. His posture was rigid. His face turned away as Charlie passed.

Then the man walked off without a word.

Charlie reached the storeroom and sat for a time, turning the pieces over in his mind. The clearing. The burned scraps. The ledger page. And now the stares.

Someone in Blowville wanted their questions buried.

When dusk settled, Charlie headed toward the first pig's ear, the quiet one. Lantern light leaked through the warped boards of the workshop. The muffled sound of cards and low voices pressed against the cold.

He reached for the door.

Something cut the air.

A knife struck the snow at his feet, blade-first, shivering with the force of the throw.

Charlie's head came up.

A man stood between two sheds, half-silhouetted by a lantern behind him. Coat collar raised. Hat pulled low. He did not advance. He lifted one hand and pointed to the knife, then toward the freight sheds beyond.

A warning.
Deliberate.
Unmistakable.

Charlie held the man's gaze until the figure turned and vanished into the dark.

He crouched, lifted the knife, turned the blade once in his hand. Sharp. Recently honed.

"Charlie."

He turned. Sarah approached from the road, breath rising in pale clouds, her eyes already searching his face.

"You all right," she asked.

"Someone doesn't want us looking any further," he said.

Her gaze dropped to the knife, then shifted past him to the freight yard, to the dark shapes of the sheds where Barclay's pig's ear hid behind ordinary boards. "Then we're closer than I thought."

"Let's step inside," Sarah said, nodding toward the quiet pig's ear, "before we draw more attention."

They moved toward the door.

Behind them, the night settled deeper between the sheds, the cold thickening like something that had decided to wait.

46

Joseph Barclay

November 24 (night), 1898 - Blowville

The pig's ear was quieter than most nights, its lanterns turned low so the shadows along the walls kept their shape. Sarah and Charlie took a small table near the stove where the heat drifted just far enough to blunt the cold without chasing it away.

Sarah ordered whiskey with a nod. The barkeep poured without comment. She drank it straight. No hesitation. No flinch.

Charlie watched, mildly surprised. "You handle that well."

Sarah set the glass down. "Fee's house had men coming through with bottles they were not supposed to have. I did not drink with them. But I learned early it was useful to know how to hold your ground over a glass." A thin smile touched her mouth. "A woman alone learns things that way."

Charlie nodded. She was not explaining herself. Just stating fact. It was becoming clear that very little unsettled her, whether whiskey or the truth she carried.

After a moment she slid the empty glass aside. "You ought to play. You said it helps you think."

"You sure you're all right."

"I have been all right longer than most men expected," she said. "Go."

Charlie left her at the table and joined a card game near the center of the room. Two woodsmen, a mill clerk, and a quiet man with a scar along his cheek looked up, then shifted to make room. The dealer resumed without comment.

The rhythm settled quickly. The stove crackled. Cards whispered across worn felt. Coins clinked in uneven stacks. Charlie won a modest pot, then folded twice, keeping himself at the edges of the game.

Then the door opened.

The sound itself was small. The reaction was not.

The room tightened, a hush passing through the pig's ear as if the air itself had drawn back. A man stepped inside, brushing snow from his gloves with deliberate care.

Joseph Barclay.

Charlie did not need an introduction. Authority clung to the man without effort. His coat was clean. His boots were polished despite the winter slush outside. Pale gray eyes swept the room, not searching so much as confirming what already belonged to him.

They stopped on Charlie for a moment longer than courtesy required.

Barclay pulled out a chair at the table as if it had been waiting for him. "Evening," he said. Calm. Polite. A voice without warmth.

No one objected. No one ever would.

Cards were dealt. Barclay played cleanly. Folding early on weak hands. Pressing just enough on strong ones to test the table. He did not bluff for show. He did not speak unless necessary. He watched.

Charlie matched his pace, keeping his face still and his breathing easy.

After a few hands, Barclay leaned slightly toward him. "You're Randall."

"That's right," Charlie said.

"I hear you've been walking around with questions," Barclay continued. "Asking them in places where questions don't sit well."

Charlie set a card down. "Truth has to sit somewhere."

Barclay's mouth shifted, almost a smile. "Careful. Truth is heavy here. Drop it in the wrong place and the men who keep the books will make sure the one holding it is the one that gets crushed."

The woodsmen shifted in their chairs.

Barclay glanced at his cards, folded them neatly, and gathered the pot with unhurried confidence. Then he stood.

"You should come by my place," he said, the words meant for Charlie alone. "Behind the freight shed. Men there speak more plainly than they do in here."

It was not an offer.

Barclay nodded once to the table and crossed the room. He paused near Sarah. She did not look up, only rolled the empty glass between her fingers. Barclay's gaze lingered a moment, then he stepped back into the cold.

The door closed.

The room breathed again.

Charlie played two more hands to let the moment pass, then returned to Sarah. She read his face immediately.

"What did Barclay say," she asked.

"He invited me to his shed."

"That's not an invitation," she said. "That's him letting you know he sees you."

Charlie nodded. "I'm still going."

"When."

"Tomorrow. Alone."

She took that in. Her jaw tightened, just enough to show it cost her something. "Be careful."

"I will."

They stepped out together into the night. The cold met them squarely, the mill's distant hum the only sound moving through the dark.

Tomorrow, Charlie Randall would step into Joseph Barclay's world.

47

Barclay's Pig's Ear

November 25 (afternoon), 1898 - Blowville

Morning came gray and brittle, the kind of cold that settled into a man's bones before he noticed it was there. Charlie left his rented room in the early afternoon and walked with measured purpose toward the freight yard. The clatter of men moving logs rang across the frozen ground, steady and workmanlike, but Charlie passed through without slowing.

He was not there for the yard.

Behind it stood the long, low shed.

Barclay's pig's ear.

There was no sign. There did not need to be. The boards were thicker than the others, the door reinforced, the windows boarded from the inside. It was a building meant to be known only by those already inside its circle.

A man stood near the entrance, pretending to smoke despite the wind. He gave Charlie a single look.

"You Randall," the man said.

Charlie nodded.

"Go on in."

The man did not knock. Did not open the door. His job was only to see whether Charlie turned around.

Charlie did not.

Inside, the room was dim and cold. Lanterns hung low and wide apart, leaving pockets of shadow along the walls. The stove in the corner burned weakly, its heat never quite reaching the edges. Men stood at the bar drinking in silence. Others played cards or dice, voices kept low, eyes sharper than in any room Charlie had entered since coming to Blowville.

They knew who ran this place. And they behaved accordingly.

Charlie stepped farther in. A few heads turned, then turned away. No one wanted to be seen watching too closely.

Barclay sat near the back at a small table, a ledger open before him. He did not look up until Charlie stopped at the edge of the table.

"Randall," Barclay said, as if confirming something he had already weighed. "Sit."

Charlie took the chair across from him.

Barclay closed the ledger with a deliberate hand. "You know what this place is."

"I can guess."

"Guessing is how men get buried," Barclay said. He studied Charlie, head slightly angled. "You walk into a room like this, you choose to be seen. Most men hide their dealings. You came through the front."

"That's where the door is," Charlie said.

Barclay's mouth lifted faintly. Not kindly.

"You're chasing answers," he said. "About Crane. About scrip. About a page you've never held but somehow keep circling."

"I'm looking for the truth," Charlie said. "That's all."

"Truth," Barclay repeated. "I warned you. It's heavy here. Men who lift it without knowing the weight tend to get crushed."

Charlie said nothing.

Barclay leaned back a fraction. "Crane thought he wanted more. Men like that either break ground or break themselves. Crane broke himself."

"He wrote my name in a ledger," Charlie said. "He brought me into this without my consent."

Barclay raised an eyebrow. "You didn't know him."

"No."

"Then you're luckier than most."

A thin ripple of laughter passed from a nearby table. Barclay did not look away.

"You came alone," Barclay said. "That tells me you're not a fool. And you're not scared enough to stay away."

"I'm not scared of answers."

"Then you're not scared of me," Barclay said. Not a question. A measure. "That can be useful."

Barclay opened the ledger again, turning pages slowly, as though considering whether to show something and deciding not to. He stopped near the middle.

"Crane carried scrip for me. Nothing unusual. Men carry things every day." His voice lowered just enough to sharpen it. "But Crane wanted standing. He wanted to rise above his shadow."

"And you let him."

"I let men try to carry what they think they can manage." Barclay closed the book. "Most drop it."

"Did he."

Barclay tapped the ledger once. "Crane spoke to the wrong people. Made promises he couldn't keep. Eventually he owed more than he was worth."

"Someone killed him," Charlie said.

"Someone," Barclay replied, "kills everyone in the end."

Charlie's jaw tightened. Barclay noticed.

"You want truth," Barclay said quietly. "Here's the first piece. Crane mattered only because he used your name. To the rest of us, he was just another man who climbed higher than his legs would hold."

"Why tell me this," Charlie asked.

"Because if you keep pushing, you'll either be useful to me…" Barclay said, pale eyes steady, "Or you'll force the wrong men to start looking for someone to blame. And I won't be the one they choose. So you'll join Crane."

The room seemed to pause for a breath.

Then Barclay leaned back, almost courteous. "That's all for today. Go. Think."

Charlie stood. Barclay remained seated.

As Charlie crossed the room, the men at the bar watched him with careful interest, measuring whether he was leaving by choice or permission.

Outside, the sky had darkened. Snow drifted lightly on the wind.

Charlie did not look back.

He had what he came for.

And he understood now that the next steps would cost more than any he had taken before.

48

Sarah's Discovery

November 25 (afternoon), 1898 - Blowville

Snow drifted in slow spirals across the yard of the Fee house, thinning near the porch where the wind cut sharper along the eaves. Sarah stood at the foot of the steps longer than she meant to, her gloved hand brushing the rail she had scrubbed so many times the varnish had worn smooth beneath her work.

She had not meant to come here.

But when Charlie insisted on confronting Barclay alone, the house had pulled at her like an unfinished sentence. Terrence Fee was gone. Crane was gone. And the rooms where she once listened, waited, and hoped now held a silence she had worked hard not to hear.

Inside, the air was colder than she expected. Terrence's brother had not yet come to take charge, and no one had tended the stove since Terrence died. Her breath clouded faintly as she moved down the dim hallway.

Everything was exactly as it had been left.

That was the problem.

She paused at the row of coat pegs. Fee's heavy work coat still hung where he had last placed it, sleeves stiff with old frost and wear.

Crane's peg was empty.

Sarah felt her jaw tighten.

Crane had told her he left in a hurry. Said he took nothing. Said there had been no time.

The bare peg told a different story.

She stepped into the kitchen. The table stood bare except for a single tin cup and the shallow dish where Fee kept coins for runners and small errands. She remembered Crane standing there one night, speaking quietly about how Fee had begun trusting him with those coins because he was steady. Reliable. Someone who did not lose track of things.

The dish held fewer coins than she remembered.

Fee had never miscounted.

Her throat tightened as she turned away.

In the back room, where Fee kept his ledgers and maps, the order felt wrong. The desk was neat, too neat. Fee worked in careful stacks, but he did not hide things. If he suspected wrongdoing, he brought it into the open. He once told her secrets spoiled faster than meat.

One ledger volume was missing.

Not misfiled. Removed.

She brushed her fingers along the empty space on the shelf. Crane had known this room as well as anyone besides Fee. He had spent hours here alone, claiming Fee wanted help sorting figures, checking routes, keeping things straight.

The understanding came cold and sudden.

Crane had not only lied about where he went that last night. He had lied about what he took. The realization did not arrive as shock. It arrived as confirmation, which was worse. She had been rearranging her life around a lie that never intended to include her.

Sarah crossed to the worktable. Fee's map of the northern tracts still lay there, corners weighted with stones. She remembered the afternoon Fee spread it out, tracing timber lines and payroll routes, explaining each mark aloud. Crane had stood beside him then, quiet and attentive, almost reverent.

She leaned closer.

A supply route had been marked faintly in charcoal. It ran between the tannery road and the freight sheds. A line with no practical purpose except easy access to the back buildings.

Barclay's sheds.

Fee would not have marked that line unless he suspected something.

Crane would not have noticed it unless he wanted it hidden.

Her heart struck hard once, then steadied.

Crane had been many things to her. Guarded. Clever. Careful in the ways he showed kindness. But honest was no longer a word she could claim for him.

She stepped back from the table, the cold sinking deeper into her bones. The longer she stood there, the clearer it became. Fee's trust had thinned in those last weeks. Crane's truths had thinned even faster.

She turned toward the door, pulling her coat tight, breath sharp in her chest.

Whatever Crane had been mixed up in, it had nothing to do with loyalty. Nothing to do with protection.

And nothing to do with her.

The ledger page she carried no longer felt like a warning. It felt like a confession he had never spoken aloud.

Outside, the winter sun strained weakly against the gray clouds over Blowville. Snow crackled under her boots as she stepped off the porch.

She did not look back.

Fee was gone. Crane was not the man she had loved, however briefly and foolishly. And the truth still buried in this valley now belonged to her.

Sarah set her jaw. If she wanted answers, then Barclay would be the one to give them.

49

Cullen Arrives

November 25 (evening), 1898 - Blowville

Snow thickened through the afternoon, turning Blowville's main road into a pale track of churned slush. Charlie climbed the porch steps of Sarah's boarding house and found her seated on the rail, elbows on her knees, watching the valley with a distant, tight-eyed focus.

She looked colder than the weather.

Charlie stopped beside her. "You were up at Fee's house."

She nodded once, then looked him over. "And it looks like your visit to Barclay's wasn't as bad as it might have been."

Neither spoke for a moment. Wind carried the distant clack of mill chains and the dull thump of bark sleds coming down off the ridge.

"What did you learn," she asked at last.

Charlie rubbed his hands together, working warmth back into his fingers. "Enough to know Barclay wanted me there. He ran the place like a court. Cards moving. Men watching every breath I took. He talked around things more than he talked about them."

Sarah's mouth tightened. "Crane used to visit him there too."

Charlie turned toward her. "You're sure."

"No," she said. "But after today, I believe it." She shifted on the rail, her coat opening just enough to show the edge of the folded ledger page tucked inside. "I went through Fee's rooms. Not looking for answers. Just looking for something that didn't feel like a lie."

"Did you find anything."

"Not directly." She drew a slow breath. "But Fee kept his house exact. Ledgers balanced. Maps clean. He never hid things. And he never removed a volume from a shelf and left a perfect gap behind."

Charlie frowned. "Crane took one."

"Yes." Her jaw set. "And more than that. He took Fee's trust. Took mine. Whatever he carried out of that house, it wasn't something he meant to bring back."

The bitterness in her voice had sharpened since morning. No grief now. Only the steady anger of someone who had finally stopped making excuses for the truth.

Charlie started to answer, then his gaze shifted down the road.

A man had turned off the slope path near the mill. Broad shoulders. Heavy coat. Beard crusted with frost. His stride was purposeful, eyes moving over doorways and porches the way a hunter reads brush for signs of movement.

Charlie's breath thinned.

Sarah followed his line of sight. "Who is that."

"Cullen Pratt," Charlie said quietly. "He's been after me since Costello."

Her brow furrowed. "Why."

"His brother died north of Galeton," Charlie said. "Someone told him I was the reason." He shook his head. "I never knew the man. Someone used my name. Crane, most likely."

Cullen paused outside the blacksmith's shop, studying the windows. He had not noticed them on the porch. Snow drifted past him like ash.

Sarah lowered her voice. "You think he'll find you."

"Blowville's too small for him not to," Charlie said. "A day, maybe two. Depends how much noise Barclay's men make on the south end of town."

She watched Cullen move on, boots crunching through stiff snow. "You planning to run again."

"No." Charlie's voice was calm, settled. "I'm done running. But I won't walk into another fight blind."

Sarah studied him. "What do you need."

Charlie hesitated only long enough to choose his words. "Fee kept more ledgers. More notes. If I'm going to show Cullen who really used my name, I need proof. Not guesses."

"You want me to go back up there," she said, already knowing.

"You know that house better than I ever will," Charlie said. "You know Fee's habits. What belongs. What doesn't. If Crane left a trail, it'll be in what he disturbed, not what he said."

A breath of wind lifted a strand of hair across her cheek. She tucked it back with a steady hand.

"I'll go tonight," she said. "If there's anything left that ties Crane to Barclay, I'll find it."

Charlie nodded. "I'll keep clear of the main road. Pratt's still hungry for answers he doesn't have."

Sarah looked down the street again, watching Cullen's figure recede into the falling snow. "He carries grief like a blade," she said.

"Yes," Charlie replied. "But maybe the truth will dull it."

Snow thickened. The porch groaned softly beneath the shifting wind.

Somewhere behind the freight sheds, Barclay's place would be waking for the night. Somewhere ahead, Cullen Pratt was drawing closer.

Sarah rose from the rail. "Go," she said. "Before he circles back this way."

Charlie stepped off the porch and pulled his collar up against the cold.

Behind him, Sarah remained still until he vanished around the corner. Then she turned toward the ridge path leading back to the Fee house.

Darkness was settling over Blowville, and the valley was moving, slowly and inevitably, toward a reckoning.

50

The Paymaster Behind It All

November 25 (evening), 1898 - Blowville

Dusk settled early in winter, and by the time Sarah reached the ridge path, the light had thinned to a bruised blue. Snow made little sound beneath her boots. Fee's house stood ahead, dark against the trees, its porch half buried beneath drifts gathered overnight.

She pushed open the door, stepped inside, and closed it behind her. The house felt colder than it had that morning. Still, like something sealed and left behind.

Sarah lit a lamp.

The warm pool of light spread across the empty kitchen table, catching dust motes drifting in the air. She moved with purpose now, not sentiment. The last of her illusions about Crane had been scraped away. She was finished remembering him as the man she wished he had been.

Now she needed truth. The kind men buried in ledgers and numbers when words worked too hard to hide it.

She crossed into Fee's study, set the lamp down, and opened the drawer she had not checked earlier. The metal lock, stiff with cold, gave way after two firm pulls.

Inside lay three ledger volumes.

Not Crane's missing one. Not the book taken from the shelf.

These were the older ledgers Fee used to track mill debts, bark yard tallies, and wages owed. Sarah lifted the top volume and flipped through pages inked in Fee's precise, compact hand.

Straight columns. Balanced figures. Honest books.

Nothing out of place.

The second ledger told the same story. A decade of wages for crews long gone. Occasional margin notes where Fee corrected a count or reminded himself to speak to a foreman.

Normal.

The third ledger was newer, covering the last year through early autumn. Sarah opened it expecting the same careful order.

But here, the pattern broke.

Fee's handwriting remained steady until mid October. After that came changes. Short, clipped notes. Margins left blank where he usually recorded questions and confirmations. Missing annotations. A faint strain in the pressure of the ink.

Sarah turned a page.

Then stopped.

A name had been written and scratched out so hard the quill had torn the parchment.

C. Randall.

Her breath caught.

Beneath it, Fee had written the name again, smaller this time, as if testing whether it belonged there.

Beside it was a brief notation.

Inquiry from P.M. re discrepancies.

P.M. Paymaster.

Sarah sat back.

Fee had spoken with the Goodyear paymaster.

She turned the page. More notes followed.

Scrip missing before arrival.
P.M. claims crew miscounted.
Does not add up. Must verify by week's end.

Her pulse thudded in her ears.

Fee had not accepted the explanation. He had been digging. Looking for the truth behind missing scrip. And someone had connected Charlie's name to the problem long before Charlie ever set foot in the valley.

She turned another page.

Then another.

The final entry, dated October 18, stood alone.

Crane meeting someone at freight shed.
Barclay involved.
P.M. instructing adjustments without record.
Speak to Hart. Quiet.

Sarah closed the ledger slowly.

The Goodyear paymaster was not careless. He was deliberate. Directing the thefts. Using Barclay. Using Crane. And somewhere along the line, Charlie Randall's name had been pulled into the books as cover.

She extinguished the lamp and tucked the ledger beneath her coat. The house swallowed her footsteps as she left.

Down the ridge path, the lights of Blowville flickered through the trees. A faint clang from the mill echoed across the valley. Somewhere in that darkness, Barclay was already settling in for another night of business.

And somewhere closer, Charlie was waiting.

* * *

She reached the boarding house porch and saw him seated on the steps, elbows on his knees, watching the road as if expecting trouble to rise out of the snow at any moment.

He stood when he saw her.

"Well," he said quietly.

Sarah handed him the ledger. "The paymaster is behind it."

Charlie's brow tightened. "You're certain."

"Yes." Her voice did not waver. "Fee suspected him. Crane met Barclay under his direction. And your name was already part of the conversation before Crane ever forged it into a ledger."

Charlie took the book carefully, as if it might come apart in his hands.

"This is proof," Sarah said. "Pratt will need to see it. And Barclay will not like that it still exists."

Snow began to fall harder, thickening the air between them.

Charlie closed the ledger and looked toward the freight sheds where Barclay held court. "Then tomorrow," he said, "we finish this."

The valley felt poised on a wire.

And as the evening deepened, trouble began to move in earnest.

51

Closing In

November 26, 1898 - Blowville

Snow kept falling through the night, thinning to a restless drift by morning. Charlie left his rented room above Barnes's shop before first light, hoping the early hour might buy him a measure of anonymity. Blowville was too small to hide in, and every hour felt like the walls of the valley were inching inward.

He stayed off the main road, moving behind sheds and stacked lumber, watching mill hands arrive for the day shift. They trudged through the cold in heavy coats, heads down, not noticing him or choosing not to. Either way, Charlie felt the weight of unseen eyes. Towns like this always watched their own.

By midmorning he had circled north of the mill and stopped near the row of freight sheds. Barclay's pig's ear slept behind them, shuttered until evening. Even closed, the place seemed to hold the night inside it. Charlie felt the memory of it settle in his chest, heavy and unwelcome.

He turned away and headed back toward town.

As he passed the other pig's ear, its door cracked open and a man stepped out. Not one Charlie recognized. The man lingered a moment too long, giving Charlie a look that was neither curious nor friendly. Just measuring.

Charlie did not slow.

Near the mill office, Sheriff Farnsworth stood with Deputy Stevens. Farnsworth looked worn down, frost clinging to the brim of his hat. Stevens leaned in close, murmuring something that drew a deeper crease between the sheriff's brows. Neither man stopped Charlie, but both followed him with their eyes as he crossed the street.

Word traveled faster than horses in places like this, especially when trouble was close enough to smell.

At the boarding house, Sarah stood on the porch with her coat pulled tight. The ledger was tucked under her arm. Her eyes held the same sleepless clarity he had seen the night before.

"You've been moving early," she said.

"Didn't want to draw attention."

She gave a small, humorless nod toward the street. "That didn't work. People are talking."

"About what."

"About Barclay's temper. About a stranger with a gambler's reputation arriving at the wrong moment. About a sheriff who dislikes loose ends."

Charlie leaned against the porch rail. "Is Farnsworth planning to ask me questions."

"He's planning something," Sarah said. "People can feel it."

Charlie exhaled slowly. The cold bit at his lungs. The morning felt brittle, as if one wrong move might splinter the whole valley.

"You find anything else at Fee's," he asked.

She shook her head. "Only confirmation. Crane worked with Barclay. And the paymaster stood behind it."

Charlie rubbed a hand along his jaw. "Then we're close."

"Close," she repeated, without comfort. "Close isn't safe."

A wagon rattled past, bark peelers hunched low beneath the weight of winter. One of the men pointed briefly toward Charlie before the wagon turned onto the lower road.

Charlie saw it. Sarah did too.

"You're being watched," she said.

"I know."

"And not only by Cullen Pratt."

Charlie's gaze drifted north, toward the bend of river behind the freight sheds. "Barclay's testing the edges. Watching who I speak to. Counting steps."

"He'll want the story settled before it spreads," Sarah said. "He can't afford questions."

Charlie nodded once. "But we have them anyway."

"And we need answers before someone decides we're easier to remove than to manage."

He looked at her then, really looked. Fear was gone from her face. What remained was steadiness, forged by disappointment and clarity.

"What's our next move," he asked.

"Tonight," she said, "you stay clear of Barclay and Pratt. Keep your head down. Let the town breathe for a few hours."

"And you."

"I'm going back to Fee's house. There's one more thing I want to check. Something I may have missed."

Charlie frowned. "Alone."

"Yes." Her voice was calm, certain. "Fee trusted me. He hid nothing from me. If there's another thread, it will be there."

Wind swept snow across the porch in a thin curtain.

"Be careful," Charlie said.

"You too."

They stood a moment longer, listening to Blowville move around them. Mill iron clattered. Men called out orders. Horses stamped warmth into frozen ground. All of it sounded ordinary. Beneath it, something tightened.

Something waiting.

Charlie stepped off the porch. Sarah turned toward the ridge path. Around them, the valley drew inward, narrowing its lines, pressing its secrets toward the surface.

The closing in had begun.

52

Charlie Refuses to Run

November 26 (evening), 1898 - Blowville

The sky had already gone dark when Charlie slipped behind the sheds near the mill yard, taking the long way back to the boarding house from his rented room. Snow drifted sideways across the valley, thin and restless, the kind that filled tracks almost as soon as they were made.

He kept to the shadows, skirting the lamplight spilling from shop windows. Too many ears were open now. Barclay asking questions. Cullen prowling the streets. Farnsworth and Stevens watching from the edges. He could feel the weight of it even when he saw no one at all.

He reached the boarding house as the last light drained behind the ridge. Sarah was already on the porch, snow dusting her shoulders, her breath rising pale in the cold.

"You're late," she said.

"I took the long way."

She stepped aside to let him onto the porch, then leaned against the rail, arms crossed tight against the cold. "I went through the rest of Fee's things," she said. "Nothing new. But what we have is enough."

Charlie rested his hands on the rail and looked out at the road. Two mill hands passed below, boots crunching in the snow. One glanced up at the house before looking quickly away. Even strangers seemed to know trouble had found him.

"I've been thinking," Charlie said. "The more we learn, the clearer it gets. Running won't fix this. Not for me. Not for Pratt. Not for you."

Sarah's jaw tightened. "I didn't say you should run."

"No," Charlie said. "But everyone else seems to be saying it for you."

"Barclay," she said.

"He wants the story buried."

"And Pratt."

"He wants someone buried," Charlie said.

They fell quiet. Snow gathered along the road, the valley holding its breath.

When Sarah spoke again, her voice was low. "Men like Barclay don't loosen their grip when something slips. They tighten it. You walking straight into that could be the last mistake you make."

"Maybe," Charlie said. "But leaving it alone feels worse."

He turned to face her fully. "I've run from accusations before. Let other men decide what my name meant. It never helped. This time I want the truth spoken where it can't be ignored. Barclay. Farnsworth. Pratt. Whoever needs to hear it."

"You're going back to Barclay's pig's ear," Sarah said.

"Yes."

"To confront him."

"Yes."

"You think he'll listen."

"No," Charlie said. "But he'll react. And what a man does when the walls start closing tells you more than anything he says."

Sarah looked away, her breath drifting over the rail. "You're a fool," she said quietly.

"Maybe."

She turned back, eyes sharp. "But you're not Crane. And you're not afraid to speak plainly."

The words settled in Charlie's chest. Not comfort. Recognition.

"I'll go tomorrow," he said. "When the place is full. When Barclay can't hide behind quiet corners."

"That's when he's most dangerous."

"I can't outrun this valley anymore."

A wagon passed, wheels grinding over frozen ruts. Farther down the road, voices began to rise as men gathered, the night easing into its usual habits.

Sarah stepped closer. "If you do this, you don't do it alone."

"No," Charlie said gently. "You stay out of it."

"I'm not asking."

"And I'm not agreeing."

She met his gaze. "Why."

"Because Barclay knows your face. Crane dragged you into this without your choosing. I won't let Barclay do the same."

The wind tugged at her coat. Snow caught in her hair. For a moment she said nothing.

"You're going to get yourself killed," she said at last.

"Not if the truth moves faster than the lies."

"Truth doesn't stop bullets."

Silence stretched between them, filled only by the creek's distant murmur and the muted clatter of the night shift at the mill.

Sarah stepped down from the porch. At the bottom step, she turned back, snow settling on her shoulders.

"Don't die for this valley," she said.

Charlie gave a faint, tired smile. "I'm not dying for the valley."

She nodded once, turned and walked into the snow, her shape

thinning as the wind took her. Charlie pulled his collar up and stepped into the dark. Tomorrow, he would go to Barclay. And he would not run.

Part 5

The Showdown

53

Night at Barclay's

November 27 (evening), 1898 - Blowville

Payday turned Blowville into something louder, rougher, and far less patient with the edges of the law.

By late afternoon the road had filled with loggers down from the ridge, bark peelers from the yards, and railmen whose pockets sagged with fresh scrip and coin. Teams stood steaming in the cold while men shouted orders and laughter in equal measure. Every door that could serve as a front for drinking stood open. Every corner held someone ready to collect a debt or make a new one.

Charlie stayed out of sight for most of the day, keeping to the higher paths above town. From there he watched wagons roll in and listened as the mill whistle sounded its end-of-week note, pushing still more men into the streets. The valley pulsed with restless money.

By the time the sun slid behind the ridge, there was no sense waiting longer.

If he was going to face Barclay, tonight was the night.

Back in his rented room, Charlie washed the soot and road dust from his hands and straightened his coat. He checked the inner pocket where Fee's torn ledger page lay folded sharp along its creases. It felt heavier than paper should.

He left as the first lamps in town began to glow.

The route to the freight sheds was busier than usual. Men leaned against walls passing bottles back and forth. Two woodsmen argued over a card game played on a crate. Laughter broke out near Mohan's store, followed by the brief, uneasy silence that meant someone had crossed a line.

Charlie moved through it all with his shoulders loose and his eyes quiet. He did not hurry. Men who hurried drew notice.

The freight yard loomed ahead, sheds lined up like blunt teeth against the snow. Behind them, Barclay's place burned with a softer, more dangerous light. Lantern glow leaked through warped boards. Voices rolled out in a thick, steady murmur.

The man at the door stood where Charlie expected him, coat collar raised, hat low. He watched Charlie approach without moving.

"You know the way," the man said.

Charlie nodded and took the handle.

Inside, heat struck him first.

The room was packed tight with men crowded shoulder to shoulder at the bar, shouting for refills. Others pressed around dice tables and cards. The air stank of sweat, woodsmoke, spilled liquor, and the sour closeness of too many bodies. Lanterns hung low, their light flashing off tin cups and the pale edges of cards.

Charlie stepped aside as the door closed behind him. At first no one paid him much attention. The noise was loud enough to swallow a single man whole.

Then he saw Barclay.

He sat near the far wall beneath a lantern hung slightly higher than the rest. Not at the bar. Not in the corners where shadows gathered. A place where he could see everything. Four men sat with him, cards in hand, eyes on their chips. Barclay's coat was neat, his posture relaxed, his attention seemingly fixed on the game.

Charlie let his gaze drift and slowed his breathing. Near the counter stood the Reverend, his back to the wall, tin cup in hand. He wore the same plain coat, the same composed expression Charlie remembered from Costello. Their eyes met. The Reverend gave the slightest nod.

Charlie returned it and began to move through the crowd.

Conversation thinned as he passed. No one stopped talking outright, but words shortened and glances sharpened. A stranger walking with purpose toward a man like Barclay meant something. Even the drunkest in the room could feel the shift.

By the time Charlie reached the table, Barclay had already set his cards down.

"Evening, Randall," Barclay said. His voice carried just far enough. "You took your time."

Charlie rested one hand on the back of an empty chair. "Busy day."

"Busy nights pay better." Barclay gestured to the seat opposite. "Sit. No sense standing like a man unsure of his footing."

Charlie sat. The dealer shuffled. Chips clinked softly.

"You find our town welcoming," Barclay said.

"It has its ways," Charlie replied. "And its shadows."

Barclay smiled faintly. "Shadows are where men keep what matters."

The first hand went around. Charlie folded early. The second he stayed in longer, matching bets until the pot was modest and the result unremarkable. Barclay watched him with quiet interest, like a man judging balance and grain in a piece of wood.

"Funny thing about names," Barclay said during the third deal. "They travel faster than the men who carry them. By the time a man arrives, his name's already been here a week, drinking and gambling without him."

Charlie glanced at his cards and set them down. "I've noticed."

"Some men resent that," Barclay said. "They feel wronged."

"And you don't."

"I've learned to be careful whose stories I trust."

The game rolled on. Pots rose and fell. Men pressed closer to the table, not tight enough to crowd, but close enough that breath and smoke blended into a single haze. Laughter faded. More eyes settled on the play.

At the counter, the Reverend set his cup aside. He watched without moving.

Charlie felt the room tightening. Each card placed, each coin pushed forward, sounded louder than it should.

Barclay leaned back after taking a small pot, rolling a coin between his fingers. “You came here for something,” he said. “Men don’t walk into places like this without a reason.”

“And men like you don’t invite them without one,” Charlie said.

A thin smile crossed Barclay’s face. “Fair.”

The dealer shuffled again. Barclay’s gaze stayed fixed.

“We’ll come to it,” Barclay said. “Tonight feels like a good night for truths.”

The room leaned in without realizing it.

Charlie felt the ledger page against his chest like a second pulse. He did not reach for it. Not yet. Some things had to be spoken when the moment could not be turned aside.

He picked up his new cards, aware of the men at his back, the eyes at his sides.

Outside, beyond heat and bodies, the valley lay under snow and cold stars. Inside Barclay’s pig’s ear, beneath lantern light and watchful faces, the air was thick enough to choke on.

The night had settled. The pieces were in place. The truth had not yet been spoken. But it would be.

54

Ledger Truths

November 27 (night), 1898 - Blowville

The next hand was dealt with more care, as though the dealer sensed something tightening at the table. Barclay gathered his cards without looking at them, his attention fixed instead on the door behind Charlie.

"You came in alone tonight," Barclay said. "I find that interesting."

"Most people around here travel alone," Charlie replied.

"Yes. But you," Barclay said, "have been anything but unremarkable since you arrived."

Before Charlie could answer, Barclay lifted one hand and gestured toward the entryway. The crowd parted slowly, a low ripple of murmurs spreading through the room.

A man stepped inside.

Cullen Pratt.

Snow clung to his coat. His jaw was set hard, his eyes carrying the same cold anger Charlie remembered from Costello. Cullen took in the room, found Barclay first, then Charlie.

He did not glance toward the bar or the tables.

He walked straight to Barclay's side.

Barclay motioned to the empty chair beside him. "Have a seat, Mr. Pratt."

Cullen sat without taking his eyes off Charlie.

"He came by yesterday," Barclay said evenly, "asking questions about you. I thought it only fair to invite him back."

Cullen leaned forward. "You thought you could outrun me."

Charlie did not move. "I wasn't running from you."

"Liar," Cullen said, his voice flat and heavy.

Barclay raised a calming hand, as though settling a disagreement over supper. "Let us keep our tempers. We are men of reason, are we not." He turned his gaze to Charlie. "You said you had something to show me."

Charlie let the silence stretch long enough for the room to lean in.

Then he reached into his coat.

Men shifted closer. Someone whispered. At the far wall, the Reverend straightened, his stillness sharpening.

Charlie set the torn ledger page on the table.

Barclay looked down at it, then back up. For the first time that evening, his expression hardened, just slightly.

"And what is this meant to prove."

Charlie tapped the entry. The forged name. The altered figures. "Crane wrote my name. Not me. He used it to move scrip and hide his tracks."

Cullen scoffed. "Convenient."

Barclay lifted the page and held it toward the lantern, studying the ink. A slow smile crossed his face. "Crane always did have a talent for copying another man's hand." He slid the page back across the table. "Perhaps he wanted to be you, Randall."

A murmur rippled through the room.

Charlie kept his voice level. "He used my name when it suited him. And when it didn't, he left enough confusion behind to ruin me."

"You expect us to believe this," Cullen said.

"I don't expect belief," Charlie replied. "Only attention."

He turned his head slightly. "Reverend."

The room stilled.

The Reverend stepped forward. His boots made almost no sound on the boards as the crowd parted for him.

"I saw it," he said. His voice was calm, carrying without effort. "Crane forged entries. More than once."

Cullen turned sharply. "You knew my brother. You told his story."

"I told what I knew at the time," the Reverend said. "I learned more afterward." He paused. "Crane used Randall's name in ledgers, in deliveries, in payout lists. And your brother…" He let the silence deepen. "…your brother saw something he was not meant to see."

The room drew a collective breath.

Barclay leaned back slightly, his eyes narrowing with calculation rather than alarm. "You should be careful," he said. "Accusations like these make men start counting what they'd rather keep uncounted. And once a room starts counting, it starts looking for a neck to hang it on."

"They already have," the Reverend replied.

Charlie slid the ledger page closer to Barclay. "Crane didn't choose names out of loyalty. He chose them because they were useful." He looked at Cullen. "Your brother was useful. So was I."

Cullen pushed up from his chair halfway. The men around the table stiffened.

The Reverend went on, his voice steady. "Crane did not serve Fee out of loyalty. He served himself and whoever paid him. When scrip went missing, when shipments failed to match counts, when the paymaster looked the other way, Crane made the numbers fit. And when someone asked questions, he made sure the blame fell elsewhere."

Silence spread through the pig's ear.

The dice tables had gone quiet. The bar had stilled. Every ear in the room was turned toward the table, toward the torn page and the truth laid bare upon it.

Barclay did not move. His face remained composed, but the room had shifted around him, a subtle tightening, a change in who was being measured.

Cullen's hand curled into a fist.

Charlie met his gaze. "Your brother didn't die because of me," he said quietly. "He died because of Crane."

The name fell like iron. For a moment, nothing moved.

Then Cullen stood fully, shaking with rage.

55

Cullen's Final Demand

November 27 (night), 1898 - Blowville

Cullen's chair scraped hard across the floorboards, the sound cutting through the sudden silence. He stood trembling, fists clenched, shoulders heaving with a breath he could not quite draw.

"You expect me to swallow that," he said. "You expect me to believe some dead man forged a name, killed my brother, and then vanished into the woods like a ghost."

Charlie stayed seated, hands flat on the table. "I expect you to listen."

"Listen." Cullen's voice broke sharp and ragged. "I crossed three towns, two rivers, and half a county chasing you, Randall. Folks told me you were a cheat. A runner. A man who gambled with more than cards. That story made sense."

Charlie did not move. "Your brother's blood is not on me."

"Liar."

The word cracked across the pig's ear.

Men near the wall rose from their chairs. Others crowded closer. A stool tipped and skidded across the boards. The room tightened, leaning toward violence before the first blow landed.

Barclay remained still, hands folded lightly in front of him, watching with faint interest. Near the door, his men had drifted closer together, almost unnoticed.

Cullen stepped forward, fists raised. “You show up in every town after he died. You leave just before trouble. You think I haven’t heard the stories.”

“I didn’t write those stories,” Charlie said. “Crane did.”

Cullen lunged.

The table went over. Cards and coins scattered across the floor like startled birds. Charlie caught Cullen’s arm, but the force carried them into the men behind them. A roar went up, half outrage, half excitement, and the room snapped into chaos.

A fist cracked against a jaw.
A chair splintered.
A lantern swung, its flame licking close to the rafters.

Men surged into the fight because it was there. Loggers, drunk and heavy with pay, swung at anything within reach. Bark peelers shoved for the exits. Railmen shouted, tripped, charged.

The pig’s ear became a single heaving mass of bodies, curses, boots, and panic.

Charlie slammed Cullen back against the wall. “Listen to me.”

Cullen’s eyes were wild, grief boiling into something ungovernable. He threw another punch. Charlie ducked and pinned him by the coat.

“Your brother died because he learned something he should not have seen,” Charlie said through clenched teeth.

“Shut up.”

“He saw Crane forging scrip counts.”

“You’re lying.”

The Reverend’s voice cut through the noise, quiet and immovable. “He is not.”

Cullen froze.

Even through the brawling bodies, the Reverend’s words carried.

“I saw Crane altering logs,” he said. “Changing numbers. Hiding scrip movement. I saw him meeting men behind the tanneries.

Your brother confronted him."

Cullen's breath caught.

"He did not slip in a creek," the Reverend said. "And he did not die by accident."

Cullen sagged against the wall, as if something in him had given way. His fists loosened.

"No," he whispered. "No."

Charlie eased his grip and stepped back.

Around them, the fight raged on. Bottles shattered. Men scrambled for the door. But in the small space where they stood, the noise dulled.

"He was not drunk," Cullen said hoarsely. "Luke did not drink. Everyone said he was drunk."

"That was Crane's lie," the Reverend said. "Others helped carry it."

Cullen's knees buckled. He slid down the wall and crouched in the sawdust and spilled whiskey.

Charlie watched him, chest heaving. The truth had torn away the one certainty Cullen had lived on. Hatred.

For a moment, neither of them moved.

Then a crash of breaking wood nearby startled them both. Another knot of fighters spilled across the fallen table. Someone screamed as a lantern burst, flaring before a boot stamped it out.

Charlie turned instinctively.

And that was when he saw her.

Sarah stood half-hidden behind a wooden partition near the storage crates, pressed close to the wall. Her eyes were wide, her breath faint in the cold draft pulling in from the freight door. She must have slipped inside after the fighting began.

Charlie's pulse jolted. He had not expected her here. Not in this place. Not in this chaos.

Before he could move toward her, a surge of bodies closed the gap and swallowed her from view.

But he had seen enough to know she was still inside.

And Barclay was gone. So were three of his men.

Charlie's stomach tightened.

Cullen wiped his face, still crouched on the floor. "Where is he."

Charlie scanned the room. Barclay's coat was gone. His calm posture. His measuring eyes.

"He left," Charlie said. "He used the noise."

The Reverend stepped closer. "Then he is already planning what comes next."

Charlie looked toward the door.

The cold outside.
The freight sheds.
The dark edges of the yard.

Something had shifted beyond this room.

And night in Blowville had only begun.

56

A Fire to Hide

November 27 (night), 1898 - Blowville

The fighting slowed before it stopped. Not order returning, but exhaustion settling into the bones of the room. Men staggered back from one another, chests heaving, faces split and bloodied, eyes dulled by drink and rage.

Charlie pushed through the press of bodies, searching for space enough to breathe. The air had turned thick and sour with sweat and spilled whiskey. Overturned tables and cracked lanterns made the pig's ear feel smaller, tighter, as if the walls had drawn inward.

Barclay was nowhere in sight.

That absence carried weight. It settled in Charlie's gut like something unfinished.

A cold wind slipped under the freight door and brushed his collar. It carried a smell that did not belong inside any pig's ear. Sharp. Oily. Wrong.

Pitch and lamp oil.

A shout rose near the entrance, wordless at first, then clear enough to cut through the din.

"Fire."

Charlie turned as a red glow crept along the seam beneath the freight door. Someone outside had tipped a lantern against the siding. Flames climbed fast, bright as a forge, licking up the pitch-soaked boards. Panic rippled through the room as men surged toward the door.

The Reverend caught Charlie's sleeve. "Barclay," he said, voice tight but steady. "He means to erase what he cannot control."

Another lantern shattered against the wall. Heat flared. Smoke rolled low along the floor before lifting in choking sheets.

Someone screamed for water. Someone else kicked at a table, trying to shove it toward the rear window.

Charlie's eyes found the storage partition. For an instant he saw Sarah there, caught in the flickering light, her face stark with fear as she tried to push against the press of bodies. The crowd surged toward the only exit not yet fully consumed.

"Sarah," Charlie called.

Two loggers slammed past him, knocking him sideways. The sound of boots and shouting swallowed his voice.

The room dissolved into noise and motion. Heat roared. Smoke thickened. The ceiling creaked as embers began to fall.

Charlie forced himself upright and shoved toward the partition. The space was empty now. She had moved, or been carried with the surge.

The freight door finally buckled outward under the weight of bodies. Cold air rushed in for a single breath before smoke swallowed the opening again. Men poured through, coughing, choking, collapsing into the slush.

Charlie followed. Flames raced along the wallboards. The fire had taken hold too quickly. Too cleanly.

He burst into the night and dropped to one knee, lungs burning as he dragged in air sharp enough to hurt.

Behind him, the pig's ear roared. The roof sagged. Fire climbed toward the eaves, painting the snow in violent orange.

Charlie pushed himself up and searched the crowd spilling into the yard. Loggers knelt retching in the snow. Others ran for buckets. Some stood frozen, staring as if the fire had stolen their understanding along with their breath.

Sarah was nowhere among them.

Charlie staggered toward the corner of the freight shed where the flames burned hottest. He shielded his eyes and stared into the glow, searching for any sign of her.

Movement cut through the smoke.

A figure stepped clear of the flames, dragging someone by the coat.

Barclay.

And in his grip was Sarah.

Her hair was singed at the ends. Soot streaked her face. Her wrists were locked in Barclay's fist, held tight as property.

Charlie's breath went thin.

Barclay saw him and smiled without warmth. The knife in his free hand caught the firelight, its edge bright and patient.

"Come any closer," Barclay said, "and she does not walk out of this town."

The wind carried the roar of the fire between them like something alive.

Charlie took a step anyway.

The night seemed to pause. And everything that had been buried beneath Blowville finally broke into the open.

57

Sarah in Peril

November 27 (night), 1898 - Blowville

The fire behind Charlie roared high enough to throw long, wavering shadows across the snow. Embers drifted like burning insects, carried on the wind up Bailey Run. Men shouted for buckets. Others stood helpless, watching the pig's ear fold inward as the heat grew too fierce to fight.

All of it fell away before the sight of Joseph Barclay holding Sarah Ebenspecker by the collar, the blade of a knife pressed close to her throat.

Charlie stepped forward, lungs still raw from smoke, ribs aching with each breath. Barclay shifted the knife just enough to warn him back.

"That is close enough," Barclay said. His voice remained steady, almost calm. Behind him, the freight shed crackled and collapsed, sparks lifting into the dark like thrown coins.

Sarah fought once, sharp and furious, but Barclay yanked her closer, the knife rising with her.

"Let her go," Charlie said.

Barclay tilted his head, studying him as if the night were a parlor and not a burning yard. "You made quite a mess tonight. You should have taken my invitation and walked away after the first drink. But you like digging."

Charlie held his ground. "You tried to burn half the town to stop a story."

"No," Barclay said. "I tried to burn one man." His grip tightened on Sarah. "Now I have reason to finish what Crane failed to handle."

Charlie felt his breath hitch at the name. Barclay noticed.

"You thought you understood his game," Barclay went on. "But you never did. Crane wanted to be me. He simply wasn't built for it."

Sarah spat blood into the snow at Barclay's feet. "Crane didn't want to be you. He wanted out. Away from you."

Barclay twisted a fist into her hair and jerked her head back. "He wanted power. He wanted respect. He lied to you as easily as he lied to everyone else."

Charlie's voice cut through the noise of the fire. "If you're trying to convince me you didn't kill him, you're wasting time."

Barclay's mouth thinned. "Crane killed himself when he touched something he didn't understand."

Charlie took another step.

The knife lifted.

"That ledger page stays buried in your pocket," Barclay said. "Whatever you found tonight, whatever you think you can prove, it ends here. Leave Blowville before sunrise and burn every scrap you pulled from Fee's house. This valley stays alive because it stays quiet. You carry that paper into daylight and the wrong eyes turn this place inside out. If you don't burn it, you won't make it past the bridge."

Charlie breathed once, slow and deliberate. "You follow me if I run. You hunt me until you catch me. And you kill us both once we are far enough from town."

Barclay's eyes hardened. "Then you understand."

Sarah's voice came low and sharp. "Charlie. Stay back."

He ignored her. "Let her go. She has nothing to do with this."

Barclay gave a short laugh. "She was Crane's shadow. She put herself where she did not belong. That makes her part of it."

Sarah shifted her weight, subtle and deliberate, tightening her stance.

Charlie saw it. Barclay did not.

She drove her elbow into Barclay's ribs. The blow landed solid, forcing a grunt from him. The knife wavered.

Charlie moved.

He hit Barclay full-force, driving him backward into the snow. The knife flew free and skittered across the frozen ground. Barclay swung wildly, calculation replaced by rage, but Charlie pinned one arm and drove a fist into his jaw.

Barclay bucked and twisted, tearing free long enough to seize a broken length of crate wood. He swung hard, catching Charlie across the shoulder.

Pain flared white. Charlie staggered, turning just in time to see one of Barclay's strongmen charging in, blade held low.

Charlie braced.

The blow never came.

Cullen Pratt slammed into the man from behind, sending both of them tumbling into the snow. The knife spun away. Cullen rose first, blood on his lip, fury burning clean and focused now, no longer blind.

"You are not touching him," Cullen said.

Another shape emerged through the drifting smoke.

Sheriff Farnsworth.

Deputy Stevens ran at his side, lantern held high. Both men took in the scene in a single, difficult breath.

"Hold it right there," Farnsworth shouted.

Barclay froze, chest heaving, blood streaking his cheek, snow clinging to his coat. Charlie still hovered over him, half-poised to strike again.

Sarah staggered back to Charlie's side. Soot marked her face, her breath shaking but steady. She laid a hand on his arm.

Farnsworth stepped closer, rifle angled but not shouldered. "I said hold."

For the first time all night, the world went still.

Behind them, the fire hissed and collapsed inward as the last of the roof gave way. Snowflakes drifted through the smoke, glowing orange before vanishing into black.

Charlie straightened, breath ragged. Sarah steadied him.

Barclay looked up at the sheriff, hatred simmering beneath the soot. "You have no idea what you are stepping into."

Farnsworth did not blink. "I know enough."

Deputy Stevens stepped in and took Barclay by the wrists.

The night finally settled.

But Blowville would carry its marks for a long time yet.

58

Barclay Falls

November 28 (morning), 1898 - Blowville

The flames of the collapsed pig's ear smoldered low now, reduced to a deep bed of coals that pulsed like a dying heart. Snow around the ruin had melted into gray slush. A dozen men stood in the cold, shivering and coughing, trading stunned looks. No one spoke above a murmur, as if raising a voice might wake something that ought to stay buried.

Deputy Stevens bound Barclay's wrists tight with leather straps before hauling him to his feet. Barclay did not resist, but his eyes never left Charlie. Not once.

"You think this ends with me," Barclay said as Stevens shoved him forward. His voice was low enough that only Charlie, Sarah, Cullen, and Farnsworth could hear. "But you do not understand the kind of men who run these mills."

Sarah stepped closer, chin lifted despite the soot streaking her face. "We understand enough."

Barclay's smile was small and grim. "Fee thought he did too."

"That is enough talk for tonight," Farnsworth said.

Stevens pulled Barclay toward the road, where two more deputies from the patrol camp were arriving with lanterns. Barclay's boots dragged through the snow, leaving uneven lines that the wind began to erase almost immediately.

Only when Barclay was out of earshot did Farnsworth turn fully toward Charlie and Sarah.

"You two had better start talking," he said.

Charlie took a breath, glanced once at Sarah, then stepped into the lantern light. His coat was burned at the shoulder, his face dark with soot. Sarah looked much the same. Exhausted. Shaken. Still standing.

"We found ledgers," Charlie said. "In Terrence Fee's house. Records Crane helped keep. They track the movement of Goodyear scrip."

Sarah continued without hesitation. "Crane was altering entries. Barclay handled distribution. But they were not working alone."

Farnsworth's brow furrowed. "You are telling me the man in Austin. The paymaster. He is tied to this."

"Yes," Sarah said. "Directly."

Before Farnsworth could respond, the Reverend stepped into the edge of the lantern light. He held out a bundle wrapped in cloth. Farnsworth hesitated, then unfolded it.

Inside lay fragments of ledger pages. The handwriting was precise. The ink steady. The alterations unmistakable.

"I brought what proof I could," the Reverend said. "This is Crane's hand. And the figures move in one direction only. Upward. Toward Austin."

Farnsworth studied the pages for a long moment, his expression hardening with each line.

"Stevens," he called.

The deputy jogged back, leaving Barclay in the custody of two patrolmen.

"Get to the office. Telegraph Sheriff Wilkes in Austin. Tell him to detain the Goodyear paymaster immediately and seize every book and ledger in his possession. Understood?"

"Yes, sir."

Stevens ran.

Farnsworth exhaled slowly, steam rising from his breath. "I should have seen this sooner. Too many strange payments. Too many quiet rumors from the camps." He gestured toward the burned ruin, the stunned crowd, the state of Charlie and Sarah. "This is what happens when the law is stretched thin."

Cullen shifted nearby, arms crossed tight, eyes fixed on the dark where Barclay had been taken. "What about Crane?"

Farnsworth looked at him with a mix of sympathy and regret. "If Crane forged these figures, he was part of it. If he disappeared…" He paused. "Some men vanish because they choose to. Others because someone chooses for them."

Cullen's jaw tightened. He said nothing.

The wind picked up, carrying fresh snow from the ridge. It fell more gently than before. Charlie felt it melt against the heat still lingering on his face.

"You both need rest," Farnsworth said at last. "Come to the office tomorrow. I want every detail. This will be finished properly."

He turned away, issuing orders as he went. Townsfolk spread through the wreckage, stamping embers, checking for the injured, guiding the last stragglers away from the ruins.

For a moment, Charlie and Sarah stood side by side, watching the fire sink into ash.

Cullen stepped toward them. His voice was quieter now, stripped of its edge. "This does not bring Luke back." His breath shook. "But it tells me where the blame belongs. I thank you for that."

Charlie nodded. Cullen turned and walked into the dark, a man without his rage for the first time in years.

Sarah touched Charlie's arm. "You are hurt."

Charlie looked down. Blood seeped through the torn fabric at his side. He had not noticed it until now.

"I will be all right," he said.

"You will be if you let me stitch that."

He managed a tired smile. "I did not know you sewed."

Her answer was a faint, humorless smile. "Fee did not mend his own clothes."

They walked away from the burned pig's ear together, leaving the hushed crowd behind them. The ruin collapsed inward on itself, smoke thinning as dawn edged closer.

Behind them, Blowville's shadows shifted. The truth had begun to surface.

And in the space where Barclay's power had stood, something quieter settled into the cold December air.

The valley was only beginning to breathe again.

Part 6

Resolution

59

The Paymaster Confession

November 28 (midday), 1898 - Blowville

A gray morning settled over Blowville like a damp wool blanket. Smoke still drifted from the freight yard where Barclay's pig's ear had burned the night before. Snow had fallen lightly before dawn, muting the world and covering the worst of the wreckage.

Charlie and Sarah walked the road side by side, speaking little. Charlie kept his coat pulled tight, ribs aching with each breath. Sarah moved with the careful stillness she took on when she was holding herself together by force of will alone.

The sheriff's office sat near the heart of town, its windows glowing faintly with lamplight. When they stepped inside, heat met them at the door, thick with the smell of coal smoke and damp wool. Sheriff Farnsworth stood behind his desk, sleeves rolled, hair rumpled from a night without sleep.

Deputy Stevens lay stretched out on a narrow cot in the corner, one boot off, the other still on, a testament to how fast the night had moved.

Farnsworth looked up. Fatigue had carved deep lines beneath his eyes, but his posture remained firm.

"You came early," he said.

"We thought you would want to speak with us," Sarah replied.

"I do." Farnsworth rubbed the back of his neck. "Sit down."

They took the two chairs opposite the desk. Sarah folded her gloved hands in her lap, fingers tight. Charlie watched her for a moment before turning his attention back to the sheriff.

Farnsworth picked up a folded telegram, tapped it once against the desk, then opened it.

"Wilkes in Austin questioned the paymaster through the night," he said. "The man broke before the first lamp burned out." He lowered the paper. "He admitted everything. Every part of it."

Sarah's breath caught, but she did not move.

Charlie spoke quietly. "What did he say?"

Farnsworth leaned forward, elbows resting on the desk. "He admitted to stealing scrip from the Goodyear payroll for years. He called it 'covering a shortage' at first, like if he kept the numbers clean no one would look too close at him. Then he learned how easy it was, and how hard it was to stop. Small amounts at first. Enough to go unnoticed. When Barclay became involved, it grew larger. Organized."

He paused, eyes steady.

"Crane was meant to take the blame if it ever came apart."

Sarah stared at him, her expression flat in a way that made Charlie's chest tighten.

"Crane," she said softly. "Of course."

"He was careless," Farnsworth continued. "Left handwriting where he should not have. The paymaster decided that made him useful. Someone to point to when the fire got too hot."

Sarah's voice came out tight but controlled. "What about my father?"

Farnsworth hesitated. The pause told Charlie more than the words that followed.

"George Ebenspecker asked questions," the sheriff said. "Honest ones. He noticed timing that did not line up. Count sheets off by just enough to trouble a decent man."

Sarah swallowed, her gaze fixed on the desk.

"The paymaster ordered two men to follow him on his walk home," Farnsworth went on. "He told them to make it look like a drunken fall. They struck him from behind with a rock, dragged him to the creek, and left him there."

Sarah's hand slipped from the edge of the desk. The sound was small, just the dull tap of knuckles against wood, but it stopped the room. She did not cry. She did not speak. Her shoulders drew in slightly, as if the air had gone thin, and for a moment Charlie thought she might fold where she stood. He did not reach for her. He stayed still, letting the silence hold what words could not.

Farnsworth set the telegram aside. "He confessed to that without being pressed. Said he regretted nothing except getting caught."

Sarah closed her eyes once. When she opened them again, they were wet but steady.

"And Crane," she asked. "What did he know?"

"Crane was told afterward," Farnsworth said. "The paymaster wanted him frightened. Dependent. By then Crane was already involved. Already forging figures. Already too deep to pull free."

Snow tapped softly against the window. No one spoke for a long moment.

Charlie looked at his hands, then at Sarah. Her jaw was tight, her shoulders trembling almost imperceptibly.

Farnsworth continued, quieter now. "As for you, Charlie, the paymaster admitted Crane chose your name because it traveled easily through the camps. A gambler. A man no one could trace. Easy to blame. Easy to lose."

Charlie felt a slow heat gather behind his breastbone.

Sarah spoke again, her voice thin but clear. "So Crane used Charlie's name because it meant nothing. The paymaster used Crane because it was convenient. And my father died because he asked the wrong question at the wrong time."

"Yes," Farnsworth said. "All of that is true."

Sarah drew a shallow breath, her fingers gripping the edge of the desk.

“Where is the paymaster now?”

“Locked in the Austin jail,” Farnsworth replied. “He will stand before the court come spring. But I do not expect he will see another summer.”

Sarah nodded once, controlled and precise. “Thank you, Sheriff. For telling us.”

Farnsworth stood. “I am sorry, Sarah. Truly. Your father deserved better from this valley.”

She rose but did not answer. Charlie stood with her.

Outside, Sarah pressed one hand to the porch rail and let out a breath so faint it almost vanished in the cold air.

Charlie remained beside her without touching. She was standing at the edge of something vast, and he knew better than to pull her away before she was ready.

When she spoke again, her voice was calm.

“I would like to go to Fee’s house.”

Charlie nodded. “I will walk with you.”

They set off down the snowy road together, the truth of the valley trailing behind them like a long shadow.

60

Sarah's Unraveling and Resolve

November 28 (afternoon), 1898 - Blowville

The snow had thickened by the time Sarah and Charlie reached the old Fee house. Drifts softened the yard and fence posts into rounded shapes, as though the world were trying to dull the sharpness of everything that had come before.

Sarah stopped at the gate. For a long moment she did not lift the latch.

"I used to think this place held answers," she said. "Now I know it only ever held reminders."

Charlie waited. In the weeks since meeting her, he had learned that the silence between her words mattered as much as the words themselves.

She opened the gate and walked up the path, boots sinking slightly into the snow. Charlie followed at a respectful distance.

Inside, the air felt untouched. Colder than outdoors. It still carried the faint, stale scent of the last fire Fee had lit in the stove. Dust lay on the mantel and table, as if the house had been holding its breath since October.

Sarah moved through the entryway slowly, her fingertips grazing the wall where she once hung Fee's coat.

"I did not come here for comfort," she said softly. "Even when Fee was alive, this house was never warm. But I learned things here. I learned how men speak when they think the room belongs to them."

She stepped into the kitchen and paused by the table where she had served Fee his meals. Her fingers followed the worn grain of the wood.

“He trusted me, in his own way,” she continued. “Or maybe he did not. Maybe he only trusted that the house would run the same every day.”

Charlie leaned against the doorway, arms loose at his sides. “What did you come back for today?”

Sarah drew a slow breath before answering. “Finality.”

She turned and walked down the hall toward Fee’s study. The door creaked when she pushed it open. The room was dim. The desk sat exactly where it always had, the chair slightly askew, as if someone had stood up in a hurry.

Even the broken drawer, the one she had once fixed with a strip of cut leather, hung open by an inch.

She stepped inside.

“I keep thinking there should be something here,” she said. “Something that explains why all of this happened. Why my father died. Why Crane became who he did. Why there is so much rot under every quiet corner of this valley.”

Her voice tightened. “But there is nothing. Just walls and old paper. And the echo of choices other people made.”

She had thought understanding would feel like relief. Instead, it felt like standing upright without something to lean against.

Charlie entered the room and stopped beside the desk, hands in his pockets. “You learned the truth. That is more than most people ever get.”

“That truth cost me three years,” she said, sharper now. “Three years moving from town to town. Three years hearing lies because men were afraid to admit what they had allowed. And a year trying to hold on to an image of Crane that was never real.”

She placed both palms flat on Fee’s desk. Her shoulders trembled, though her breathing stayed controlled.

“Crane lied to me,” she whispered. “He used me. He helped the men who killed my father. And I kept a place for him in my heart, even when I knew something was wrong."

Charlie stepped closer. "You were looking for someone to trust."

"I was looking for someone to tell me the truth," she said. "And Crane was the closest thing I had."

She bowed her head, eyes fixed on the scarred surface of the desk. Snow tapped faintly at the window. The silence pressed in, as though the house itself were listening.

After a long moment, she straightened. Her face was pale, but steady.

"I cannot stay here," she said. "Not in this town. Blowville was never mine. I came because I had nowhere else to go. I stayed because I needed answers. Now that I have them, there is nothing left for me here but ghosts."

Charlie nodded slowly. "Where will you go?"

"I do not know yet," she said. "But when I leave, it will be my choice. Not something forced by fear or grief."

She moved to the window and looked out at the falling snow. The yard lay quiet, fence posts softened, the road beyond nearly erased.

When she turned back to him, her expression had settled.

"Thank you," she said.

Charlie blinked. "For what?"

"For being honest when everyone else chose to lie. For staying today. For not telling me how I should feel." She paused. "You gave me that space, whether you meant to or not."

Charlie shifted, unsettled by the weight of her gratitude. "You did not need someone to tell you what to feel. You already knew."

A small, sad smile touched her mouth.

She walked past him, steps measured, and paused again in the kitchen. Charlie followed her outside and closed the door behind them. The house settled back into silence.

At the bottom of the steps, she stopped and faced him.

“I am not leaving today,” she said. “But I will leave soon, once I understand what comes next.”

Sarah reached into her coat pocket and paused. Her fingers closed around the small locket she had been carrying, the chain worn thin where it had rubbed against her skin. For a moment she stood still, weighing it, then stepped back to the porch rail and set it down. She did not open it. She did not look at it again. When she turned back to Charlie, her expression had settled into something quieter and firmer than before.

“And you? Where will you go now that this is finished?”

He looked toward the snow-covered road, the valley stretching quiet and uncertain.

“I have a few ideas,” he said. “Nothing settled.”

That seemed enough for her.

They started toward the boarding house together, the cold closing in around them without urgency.

For the first time since arriving in Blowville, Sarah’s steps were not pulled backward by the past.

They were steps taken forward.

61

Cullen's Closure

November 28 (evening), 1898 - Blowville

By the time Sarah and Charlie reached the boarding house, the snowfall had eased into a fine drifting powder. Light clung to the treetops above Blowville, turning the valley silver. The air carried the smell of cold bark and spent chimney smoke. It was the kind of winter evening that felt suspended between two breaths.

Sarah slowed near the porch steps. Charlie walked beside her, hands deep in his pockets, his bundle hanging loose from one shoulder.

"I should let you rest," he said. "It has been a long morning."

"Rest," Sarah murmured. "I do not even remember what that feels like."

Charlie was about to answer when another sound reached him. A horse's snort. The soft creak of saddle leather.

Across the road, Cullen Pratt stood beside his mount at the hitching post, tightening the straps on a bedroll. Snow dotted his coat. His expression was distant, settled, stripped of the wild heat that had driven him these past weeks.

He looked up and saw them. For a moment, none of the three moved.

Then Cullen adjusted the reins and stepped toward them.

The last time Charlie had seen him, Cullen had been standing in the wreckage of a fight, chest heaving, rage split open by truth.

Now he walked with a deliberate calm, as though the grief inside him had settled into something he could finally carry.

“Randall,” he said quietly.

“Pratt.”

Sarah gave a small nod. Cullen returned it with a respectful lift of his chin.

“I am leaving town,” he said.

Charlie nodded. “Seems right.”

Cullen let out a breath that might have been a laugh, but lacked the sound for it. “I thought I would feel something when I learned the truth. Relief. Satisfaction. Maybe even peace. Turns out all it did was leave me empty.”

Sarah spoke gently. “Truth often does. It takes more than it gives.”

Cullen looked at her, then back to Charlie. “I chased you across half this county. Told myself you were the man who ruined my life.” He shook his head. “Turns out you were the only one not lying.”

Charlie shifted his weight. “I did not do much.”

“You did enough,” Cullen said. He hesitated, searching for words. “I built myself around that chase. Around the need to make someone pay. I do not know who I am without it.”

Charlie studied him a moment, then spoke in the same even tone he used at a card table when the stakes were real.

“Go somewhere you are not known,” he said. “A place that does not remember you before you arrive.”

Cullen took that in slowly. “You think that works.”

“I know it does,” Charlie said.

Cullen nodded once. “Then I will try.” His gaze drifted back toward the road. “There is nothing for me here except what I already buried.”

He turned toward his horse, then paused and faced Sarah again.

"I am sorry about your father," he said. "Truly."

Her expression softened. "And I am sorry about your brother."

Cullen dipped his head, then swung into the saddle with practiced ease. He looked down at Charlie one last time.

"Take care of yourself," he said.

Charlie answered with a small smile. "I intend to."

Cullen turned his horse down the main road, past the mill yard and the blackened remains of Barclay's pig's ear. Soon he disappeared between the tall pines along the southern trail.

Sarah watched until the trees swallowed him.

The quiet that followed was heavy, but not painful. It was the kind of quiet that comes when something long unresolved finally settles.

Charlie turned toward her. "I will be leaving soon too."

She looked at him, considering the words before answering. "I thought you might."

He adjusted the strap of his bundle. "You helped clear my name. Helped me see what Crane had done. I am grateful."

"And I am grateful you stayed," she said. "When you did not have to."

A faint, bittersweet smile touched her mouth.

Charlie touched the brim of his hat in a small gesture. "Take care of yourself, Sarah."

She drew a breath, stepped forward, and wrapped her arms around him. The embrace was gentle, then steadier. Charlie rested a hand at her back and closed his eyes.

When she pulled away, she did so with a quiet certainty he had not seen in her before.

Without another word, she turned and went up the steps, disappearing into the boarding house. The door closed softly behind her.

Charlie stood on the porch a long moment, watching the snow drift down, letting the weight of the valley settle without resistance.

Tomorrow, he would leave Blowville. But tonight, the world was still. And for the first time in months, he allowed himself to feel it.

62

Charlie Walks Out of Blowville

November 29, 1898 - Blowville

Snow fell in the thin, weightless way it sometimes did when the world wanted to be quiet.

Charlie stepped out of the storehouse room as dawn began to gather over Blowville. What light there was came pale and silver, brushing the roofs of the mill cabins and the tops of the hemlocks surrounding the town. His breath drifted ahead of him as he descended the narrow steps, bundle slung over one shoulder, hat pulled low.

The night had been still. Too still. After the fire. After Barclay's fall. After the truth had finally forced its way into the open.

He paused in the road and looked around. Blowville was not a dying town. It still throbbed with the energy of a place built on labor and want. The sawmill would be running by midmorning. Teamsters would shout across the yards. Bark men would stack hides near the sheds. The place would groan and shudder awake as it always had.

But there was something else now. A weight. A breath being held. Charlie felt it settle somewhere deep and steady inside him, as if the town had pressed something into him and left it there.

He walked toward the Mohan General Store, boots crunching softly in the fresh snow. The windows glowed faintly with the first stirrings of the day. When he stepped inside, warmth struck his face and brought with it the smell of coffee and flour.

Mr. Mohan stood behind the counter, beard gone mostly white, eyes clear and unhurried. He nodded as if greeting a man he had known far longer than a handful of days.

"You heading out this morning," Mohan said.

"Seems so," Charlie replied.

Mohan slid a biscuit wrapped in paper across the counter. "For the walk."

Charlie placed a coin down. Mohan pushed it back without looking at it.

"Just take it."

Charlie hesitated a moment, then nodded his thanks and took the biscuit. The warmth of it settled into his hand, small but real.

He stepped outside again. Across the road, the boarding house sat quiet, its porch lightly dusted with snow. He saw no movement behind the windows, but the place felt awake to him all the same, as if it were watching him leave.

He started walking. The road bent gently toward Bailey Run, following the water's slow twist east. Snow muted everything. Even the stream sounded softer beneath its thin lid of ice.

Charlie walked with an easy, even stride. His shoulders were loose, his hands relaxed in his pockets. The cold pinched his ears and fingertips, but he welcomed it. It felt clean. Honest. The kind of cold that asked nothing in return and gave no false comfort.

After a time, he glanced back.

The valley spread out behind him. Cabins rose from the snow. Smoke curled from chimneys. The mill wheel stood dark against the white. It was not the most beautiful place he had known. Not the safest. Not the kindest.

But it had been a turning. It had shown him what names could be used for. What men became when they hid behind them. What lies cost. What truth demanded.

In one of the upstairs windows of the boarding house, a shape shifted.

Sarah stood behind the thin curtain, her face pale in the glass, eyes fixed on the road.

Charlie slowed, just enough. He lifted a hand.

She did not move at first. Then she raised her own, slow and deliberate. The gesture carried no pleading, no regret. It was a farewell shaped by resolve, the kind that did not ask to be answered.

Charlie held it a moment longer than he needed to, then let his hand fall. He turned back to the road.

He reached into his coat pocket and flicked a playing card between his fingers. A jack of hearts. It spun once, twice, catching the light like something remembered rather than forgotten. He watched it settle, then tucked it away and kept walking.

Maddy would have called him Charlie, and meant it. For the first time in a long while, the name he carried no longer felt like something borrowed or taken. It had not come back to him clean. Too many hands had held it. Too many men had spoken it for the wrong reasons.

He thought of Cullen Pratt in the firelight. Of Sarah standing steady when the truth came due. Of the men who had never had the chance to set their own names right.

A name, he understood now, was not something a man carried alone. It gathered weight from every place it had been, and every man who had tried to use it.

His name felt like his again. Not because it had been returned to him. Because he had chosen to keep it.

Someone had mentioned Cross Fork once. Logging camps. Quiet games. Nothing reckless. Nothing cruel. Just enough to keep a man sharp. It sounded like the right direction.

Charlie drew in a breath, tasting pine, smoke, and the deep cold that settled into everything this time of year. The air held steady in his chest before he let it go.

Then he walked on, leaving Blowville behind.

Bailey Run murmured beside him. Snow drifted down without hurry. The world opened ahead, pale and wide.

And Charlie Randall stepped into it with the steady stride of a man who had seen what a valley could hide and still believed there was room ahead for whatever came next.

www.ingramcontent.com/pod-product-compliance
Lightning Source LLC
LaVergne TN
LVHW100521110826
845146LV00002B/731

* 9 7 9 8 9 9 3 9 8 4 9 5 7 *